William Jackson

William Jackson is a British author of gay horror fiction. His characters inhabit a homonormative world in stark contrast to the heteronormativity of so much horror narrative. His writing looks at oppression, the inherent seductiveness of evil and the corruption, or moral decay, masked by beauty. Often evoking the atmosphere of classic Amicus and Hammer horror films, his cinematic style has been described as *Hammer horror for the 21st Century*. He cites his literary influences as James Herbert, Dennis Wheatley and Fred Mustard Stewart.

William Jackson is the Shirley Jackson of today.
~Valerie Leon

www.williamjackson.uk

WILLIAM JACKSON

WHO'S AFRAID OF SHIRLEY JACKSON?

INTRODUCED BY VALERIE LEON

Cambridge
Queer Press

First published in 2025 by the Cambridge Queer Press, an imprint of
MFco Ltd. Unit 4 City Limits, Danehill, Reading RG6 4UP, UK.
www.cambridgequeerpress.co.uk

ISBN 978-1-912622-58-0

Text is set in Caslon 11pt on 13pt.

for shirley jackson
1916 – 1965

thanks

I would like to thank the following people: Christina Oakley Harrington, proprietor of Treadwell's Books, for her invaluable insights into owning and running an esoteric bookstore (Persephone's, the fictional bookstore in the novel is, in the most part, based on Treadwell's); my publisher, Martin Firrell, and the team at Cambridge Queer Press – James Rice-Davies, Nathalie Crass-Fielding, Ben Hunter, Grace Onyango-Bell and Paloma Sarsgaard. Thank you to Barry Langford of Langford Associates for his expertise and charm. And, of course, thank you to Valerie Leon for her colourful and astute introduction to this volume.

introduction by valerie leon

i

From *Who's Afraid of Shirley Jackson?* I have learned that a book group can be a very dangerous place! A year after the death of her wife, Judy realises she must get on with her life and, although nervous of social occasions, she decides to join The Shirley Jackson Club, a book group which meets at an occult bookshop in Cambridge.

Her fellow members are Freya, the owner of the store who also happens to be a witch; Sebastian, a once-successful author now suffering from writer's block; and four students – Preet and Nancy, and gay couple Tom and Leon, all reading English at St Benedict's College. As these diverse characters meet to discuss and dissect that week's novel, we are drawn into their circle, learning more about their lives, loves, and fears.

Reading this ingenious and terrifying new novel, I was struck by how much the character of Judy, so doubtful of her ability to contribute to the group and in her own words something of a 'Miss Mouse', reminded me of my younger self.

When I was a young actress in the 1960s and 70s, going from film to film and leading what was considered a rather glamorous life, I am sure few people guessed just how shy and introverted I was. I rarely socialised with any of the actors I worked with; I would spend most lunchtimes alone in my dressing room, nibbling on sandwiches I had brought from home, rather than joining my colleagues merrily swapping amusing stories in the studio commissary. How I regret that now! I later learned that, because of this, I had acquired a reputation for being rather standoffish when in fact I was simply too overcome with self-doubt and shyness to join in.

ii

I have another curious connection with Judy; when she is asked for her thoughts on Shirley Jackson's *The Haunting of Hill House*, she reveals that it is only the second horror novel she has ever read. Likewise, *Who's Afraid of Shirley Jackson?* is only the second horror book I have ever read. The first was Bram Stoker's *Jewel of the Seven Stars*, which I read in preparation for my dual roles in the film version *Blood from the Mummy's Tomb* – but more of that later. I have always been a total scaredy-cat, afraid of the dark and anything remotely creepy. When I was about 16 or 17, I was gifted a copy of *The Haunting of Hill House* by one of my brothers who really ought to have known better. I'm afraid I never managed to finish it!

In *Who's Afraid of Shirley Jackson?*, the singular

atmosphere of the city of Cambridge is present throughout the novel, almost becoming another character in the unfolding horror. I have spent many happy days in this vibrant conurbation over the years and found myself recognising many of the places featured in the story such as Victoria Bridge, the Round Church, and Bridges café. But although the beauty of the city is undoubtedly captured in the book, Cambridge by night also emerges as a somewhat eerie, even sinister place, referred to as a 'little ruined city, built on depravity and death' and 'a more suitable spot for suicides than books'. How interesting this is! And it is something I will look out for next time I visit.

Since playing an evil Egyptian queen, reincarnated to wreak terrible vengeance, in Hammer's 1971 release *Blood from the Mummy's Tomb*, a film which went on to achieve cult status, I am aware that I too have become something of a horror movie cult figure. Whilst this is very flattering, it often comes as a surprise to people (if not a disappointment) that in reality I almost never watch horror films. *Blood from the Mummy's Tomb* is one of the very few I have ever seen.

iii

Once, when I was at a convention in America, I was persuaded to go to a screening of 1963's *The Haunting*, which was based on Shirley Jackson's aforementioned book *The Haunting of Hill House*. As the film was by then 40 years old, I felt it could not possibly be all that frightening and would therefore be safe for me to view. How wrong I was! Thirty minutes in, I was so overwhelmed by a feeling of mounting terror that I had

11

to make my excuses and leave. A year or two after *Blood from the Mummy's Tomb*, I was asked to meet with a director who was interested in my playing a role in a truly terrifying American horror movie. I spent days agonising over how to get out of this meeting without annoying my agent or alienating an important director who might one day offer me a job in a less scary project. I was about to feign a convenient illness when out of the blue I received an offer to shoot the bawdy comedy *No Sex Please – We're British* and because the filming dates would preclude me from working on the horror picture, I accepted with alacrity and much relief.

iv

Of the quotes William Jackson has chosen to introduce each chapter of the book, the majority are by women. What a clever way to highlight and celebrate the outstanding work of the many female writers who have contributed so greatly to the genre but are often overlooked. My close friend and Hammer horror compatriot, the late, great Ingrid Pitt, was an extremely talented writer who authored several successful books, ranging from a biography of Juan and Eva Perón to the children's adventure *Bertie the Bus*. For some reason, she was never able to secure a publisher for any of her novels in the horror genre nor to sell any of the many horror film screenplays she worked on. I have often wondered why the bewitching star of Hammer's *Countess Dracula* was denied a publisher in what seems to me the most obvious arena for both her talent and her image.

It says much for Shirley Jackson's storytelling that, 60

years after her death, her work still has the power to unnerve and inspire. I have never doubted the importance of horror fiction but, being filled with dread all those years ago by *The Haunting of Hill House*, I hadn't picked up another spine-chiller until now. I was equally frightened as I read *Who's Afraid of Shirley Jackson?* and have to confess it has given me some very sleepless nights. That said, I am immensely glad I summoned up the courage to delve into this dark and engrossing story, and I genuinely feel that William Jackson is the Shirley Jackson of today.

"A word after a word after a word is power."
MARGARET ATWOOD

chapter one

*"A most suitable spot, certainly; more suitable for suicides,
I would think, than for books."*
THE HAUNTING OF HILL HOUSE | SHIRLEY JACKSON

*More suitable for suicides
than for books.*

i

A sickening crash thunders through the house and Judy knows something awful has happened. Now she is running towards the study, and she's dreading the moment, dreading what she's going to find. Then she is confronted by the terrible truth of it; shock takes her in its quaking grip; books are strewn across the floor; the chair is on its side, its back is broken. Why hadn't Greta called her and asked her to help? To steady the damn thing? Judy cradles her wife in her arms, the woman she's shared her life with for thirty-three years.

'I'm here. You're going to be okay.' Judy speaks softly, her voice catching; her heart is thudding in her chest.

Greta isn't moving. She doesn't know if Greta can hear

her. Blood is damp in her hair, a soggy lump is growing rapidly where she's cracked her skull against the corner of her writing desk; oak, antique, horribly solid. There is a red stain on the floor. Judy runs to fetch a towel, presses it against Greta's head. Then she uses the phone.

'Which emergency service do you require?'

'Ambulance!'

She curses herself. It was all so avoidable. So bloody, bloody stupid. But then aren't all accidents 'stupid'? Greta had been talking about Gibbon's *Fall of the Roman Empire*. Ironically. Judy could laugh; shock, like grief, takes people differently. She should have known Greta would go looking for it on the top shelf. They'd been together forever, knew each other inside out. Judy should have been able prevent this.

The lunch Judy was preparing now lies abandoned in the small galley kitchen of number 94 Eden Street. The breadknife lies diagonally across on the chopping board; tea leaves wait for boiling water in a ceramic pot hand-painted with lavender flowers. Today's lunch was to have been Greta's favourite: salad sandwiches with lettuce, tomato, sliced egg, red onion, beetroot between thick-cut doorstops of wholemeal bread amply smeared with mayonnaise. The kettle, forgotten on the hob, is whistling angrily for attention. In the distance a siren is screaming its head off as it races in the direction of Eden Street.

ii

A 'little ruined city' the Venerable Bede called it. Pillaged by the Vikings. Crushed by William the Bastard. A city blighted by violence like a contagion harboured in its ancient walls. And then the real contagion, a plague of the blood, a Black Death. So many fallen bodies decaying in the damp ground. Such impenetrable blackness – Cambridge, the 'little ruined city'. Even its university was founded by men fleeing persecution; this little ruin had been their haven. They built libraries; over one hundred libraries to light up their pretty little disaster of a city; cathedrals of knowledge rising up out of violence and hate.

Ignorance is the curse of God; knowledge is the wing wherewith we fly to heaven.

Look closely, though, and you will see the evil of mankind recorded here in meticulous, educated detail on a million-million yellowed pages. A record of damnation and hot blood spilled. The blood of youth (Slaughter of the Innocents?). Here is man's base nature stripped bare and exposed for all to see: *Heart of Darkness, Lord of the Flies, The Catcher in the Rye, Slaughterhouse Five*: literary titans of depravity, brutality, and 'all hope gone'. And just the tip of the iceberg; there are many more godless books than these.

It moves closer now. Searching. A fluttering in the half-light: the erratic wings of an unholy bird of prey. If it can just find a way in.

To this most suitable of places.

A more suitable spot for suicides than for books.

This is a city of ideas and learning, of young and vital minds, the finest minds in the world, it can be claimed. And the beating wing in the half-light is the augur of their doom.

A cool breeze harries the garden of 94 Eden Street, hustling the hydrangeas and caladiums. Autumn is marching relentlessly in. The back door creaks on its hinges; the draft finds its way into the house.

A solitary red balloon drifts into the well-kept garden as if from somewhere unknown, from somewhere unimaginable. It presses against the window of the study and seems to stick there as if pausing to spy on the two women inside; one cradling the other tenderly. It rubs along the surface of the glass, almost gleefully; a fat, round, bloodthirsty flash of red. Then it lifts upwards, rising through the air, over the slate roof and away. Now it is brushing the tips of the ornamental trees in Christ's Pieces. Now it rides over the emerald lawns of Sidney Sussex College.

Cambridge – this most suitable of places. The balloon flies above the conical spire of the Round Church, once round the circumference and up, up and away into the limitless sky, its fat little body an unholy omen.

Trip no further, pretty sweeting, journeys end in lovers meeting.

Twelve months later.

Judy took a seat at the window, away from the other diners. She looked out through the wide shopfront across bustling Bridge Street to the wrought-iron gates of St John's College. Bridges was the kind of smart indy coffee house Cambridge did so well; a pleasant enough place to while away an hour or so. A place to meet a friend, work on your thesis or just sit and read the paper – or a good book. Patrons were met at the door by the smell of freshly squeezed orange juice and percolated coffee; a cosy and congenial place. There were pastries, freshly-made sandwiches, salads and vegetarian dishes. In spite of these temptations, Judy wasn't really hungry; she rarely had much of an appetite these days. All she wanted was coffee, the way she always took it: an americano with a dash of hot milk on the side. She finished her drink and tapped her empty cup distractedly with nervous fingers.

She and Greta had passed the little coffee house often enough on the way to an exhibition at Kettle's Yard but they'd never ventured inside. Two sexagenarians comfortably set in their ways; their time filled with agreeable routines and favourite haunts: lunch and a glass of wine at The Free Press; tea and Chelsea Buns at Fitzbillies or a lunchtime recital in Downing Place. All of this was fitted around Greta's tutoring programme on Greek and Roman history.

Greta had been dead almost a year now.

Judy needed to get on with her life; she'd finally accepted that, but she still couldn't face going back to any of the old places; too many sympathetic nods and smiles and phrases kindly-meant. She didn't want to be reminded that Greta was gone. When she walked around the Botanical Gardens or sat by the Cam feeding the ducks, she could pretend, at least to herself, that Greta was back at the house, marking essays or preparing for a lecture.

'You go without me today, love, I really must get these finished.'

But every morning when she woke up and turned over, she was hollowed out all over again; the empty bed, the dull, unshakeable ache of grief. People were only trying to be nice; tea and sympathy and all that. But being reminded didn't help at all. She'd really rather they just said nothing.

She realised she was sighing out loud — an old dear in a coffee shop, nothing more than that, lost in thought. She turned the book over in her hands: *The Haunting of Hill House*. Odd how the cover didn't seem to have anything to do with houses: a picture of a shadow, a woman's shadow, upside down. Why was it upside down? Nothing to do with houses at all. And that phrase the author kept repeating? 'Journeys end in lovers meeting.'

No, they don't. Journeys end in lovers dying.

The old uneasy fluttering of anticipation was back; the same feeling she had when she walked into the drab little seminar room all those years ago; so many curious (or perhaps judgmental?) faces turning to look at her. She was only eighteen, away from the comforts of home for the first time, living in a tiny bedsit in Tottenham Hale and studying English at Middlesex Polytechnic. She'd forced herself to join the Lesbian and Gay Society. She never liked that goldfish-bowl feeling, walking into a room full of strangers. But she had to do something; to live, to be alive! All these years later, after so much life lived, she found herself back in the same position; she had to do something now. You can't mope around the house forever, she'd told herself; no more tears; get on with it, go to the blasted book group. She'd meant to go the week before but her resolve had failed at the last minute. She stayed at home and listened to a play on Radio 4 instead; a dramatisation of an old Agatha Christie, *The Body in the Library*. This week though, she was taking the plunge – the book group started in ten minutes. The woman who organised it was very persistent on the phone: 'We're just starting out, really. Only been going a couple of months. There are only a few of us but we're all terribly keen. Do come!' So here Judy was. Time to bite the bullet. At least no one in the group would know about Greta; so no pitying looks, no awkward half-smiles.

'More coffee?' the waitress said, startling Judy back to the present.

'No,' she said. 'No, thank you. Just the bill.'

The waitress pointed at Judy's book. '*The Haunting of Hill House* is great. Are you enjoying it?'

Judy wasn't really sure what to say. People rarely asked her opinion; she'd never been sure how much it was worth anyway. Greta mostly asked her about the nuts and bolts of life. Shall we have salmon on Wednesday? What about getting an extra bookshelf? Should we get the windows repainted now or will they survive another winter? That was why they were so good together. That was why they lasted so long. Greta was the genius, the scholar, the professor, and Judy was the homemaker. A neat and orderly home filled with the aromas of furniture polish and good, traditional cooking. A simple partnership, a solid union, and it had continued solidly for more than three decades.

'I don't know,' Judy said to the waitress, turning the book over in her hands again. 'I haven't made up my mind yet. Are you a student?'

'Yes.'

'What are you reading?'

'History of Art,' the girl said. 'At King's. I'm in my second year.' She walked over to the cash register. She had the untarnished confidence of the very young (and the not fully rounded), an early explorer in the world, open to everything. Maybe Judy could take a little strength from that; so much ease and light shone from the souls of young people. She was probably three times the girl's age, but that didn't mean she couldn't dip her toe back in the waters of life, so to speak. Judy left a handful of coins on top of her bill and stuffed *Hill House* into her handbag.

'See you again.' The girl smiled from behind the counter. She had the brightest green eyes set in a lovely, elfin face, the guileless loveliness of youth.

'Yes… definitely.'

Judy walked out onto Bridge Street. The evening sky promised a downpour and dark spots of rain were already marking the pavement. But Persephone's Books was no more than a five minute walk away. She scolded herself for forgetting her umbrella. By the time she reached St Edward's Passage, the sky had darkened dramatically; rain was falling in urgent, heavy drops.

As if contradicting the weather, a warm glow spilled onto the rainy street from Persephone's windows. The interior looked like something from a *Harry Potter* novel and Judy recognised the pungent scent of Nag Champa. Mismatched shelves displayed old books of different shapes and sizes: volumes of magical ritual, Egyptian mythology, Theosophy (whatever that was), Wicca, Druidism, New Thought (Judy was at a loss).

The woman behind the counter was large, Afro-Caribbean with black-painted fingernails and, when she spoke, a voice that was rich and fine as golden Tussore silk. 'Are you here for the book group?'

'Yes,' Judy said, eyeing bookmarks on the counter with an eye inside a pyramid and the legend: *Persephone's Occult Bookstore*. Oh dear, she thought, one of those. I won't stay long.

'It's downstairs.' The woman nodded towards the back of the store.

A wide staircase, a short pile of books on each step, curled around and underneath the main floor of the shop. The stairs ended in a large, low-ceilinged basement that ran half the length of the shop again. In the centre was an oval table and an assortment of chairs. The woman with a great mane of grey hair, lighting black and red candles, must be the organiser, Judy thought. She wore an orange kaftan and many, many necklaces with various arcane symbols, none of which Judy recognised.

'You must be Judy.' The woman beamed, proffering a hand with an ornate ring on each finger. 'Welcome to the Shirley Jackson Club.'

Something about her put Judy instantly at ease. She couldn't have been much younger than Judy herself, maybe late fifties?

'Biscuit?' the woman said, thrusting a packet of Hobnobs in Judy's direction, biting into one herself. 'Wine?' She cast an arm towards an assortment of bottles on a trolley. 'Or herbal tea? We like to encourage a relaxed atmosphere here, let our hair down a bit. That way we can really dive deeply into the book, share our gut feelings, without judgment or inhibition.'

'I'm not sure I'll have that much to say. I haven't read the author before,' Judy said. 'Do you only ever do books by Shirley Jackson?'

'Goodness no, that would be a bit strange. It's just the name we chose for the group. We only read horror fiction, so it made sense to name ourselves after one of horror's greats.'

Horror fiction? Judy thought. Not my cup of tea at all.

'Oh, I am so sorry,' the woman said. 'I haven't introduced myself properly. I'm Freya. I own Persephone's.'

'How do you do?'

Freya looked past Judy to an elderly man making his way slowly down the staircase. 'Sebastian!' He was elegant rather than handsome with intelligent eyes and a broad smile. A scarlet-lined cape was draped theatrically over his shoulders. He had an air of unquestionable authority, a bearing reminiscent of a certain type of man from the 1930s and 40s. At first glance, he seemed, to Judy at least, quite the eccentric, quite the showman.

'You'll have a glass of something, won't you, Sebastian?' Freya seemed keen to get everyone merry, Judy thought, or maybe she was just a little nervous herself.

'I'll join you in a tipple,' Sebastian replied, that broad smile lighting up his face.

He looked Judy up and down. 'You look very familiar. Have we met?'

'I think I'd have remembered,' Judy said.

'I'm sure I've seen you round and about – with another woman, maybe?'

'Maybe. Cambridge is quite a small place, isn't it?'

'And, you don't recognise Sebastian?' Freya asked.

'Why on earth would she?' Sebastian said good-humouredly.

'Don't be so modest,' Freya scolded, nudging Judy's arm. 'This man is horror royalty.'

'I've dabbled in the genre,' Sebastian said coyly, 'in the dim and distant past.'

'Does the name S.J. Sizemore mean anything to you?' Freya asked Judy.

'I'm afraid not.'

'*Hand of Satan? Fear of the Dark? The Devil's Maidens?*' Judy shook her head.

'They're all cult books now,' Freya said, buzzing like a loose wire. 'They were published by Pan in the sixties and seventies. All of them written by this man here.'

'Congratulations,' was all Judy could think of to say.

'It was a lifetime ago,' Sebastian said with a dismissive wave of the hand.

'Are you still writing?' Judy asked.

'The last novel I published was *The Devil's Mistress*, the follow-up to *Maidens*, back in 1978. I'm afraid there's been quite a lull in my output since then. But, I've started working on something new: a novel based on devil worshippers and human sacrifice. I've been researching it fastidiously and I'm hoping to get some expert help in crafting the text.' His face lit up improbably, like a schoolboy with a titillating secret.

Lively chatter floated down the stairs followed by two young women; the first was British Asian with a marked Manchester accent, her hair in a sleek black chignon; Freya introduced her as Preet. Her companion was smaller and wore glasses. Judy guessed she must be of Northeast Asian heritage.

'I'm Nancy,' the smaller girl said. 'Bit old fashioned, I know, but my dad loves Nancy Kwan. Ergo I got lumbered.'

'I think it's lovely. Nancy Kwan was a great beauty in her day,' Judy said, at the same time wondering why these perfectly charming young women wanted to spend an evening talking about horror.

'By the way,' Preet said to Freya, 'the boys aren't coming. They're behind on their reading.'

'Meaning they haven't done any at all,' added Nancy, 'because they're always lying in bed watching David DeCoteau movies.'

'The boys, Tom and Leon, are a couple,' Freya explained. 'They're students at St Benedict's College, like Nancy and Preet.'

'English Lit,' Nancy said, rummaging in an enormous shoulder bag. 'Oh hell, I've left my copy of *Hill House* back in my room.'

'With Nancy, forgetfulness is an art form,' Preet said rolling her eyes.

Freya dimmed the lights. The candlelight swayed and flickered over the faces of the assembled group. 'Well, it seems we're all here,' she said. 'Shall we get started?'

Judy felt the chill in the room suddenly. And there it was: that uncomfortable ripple in her stomach; her breathing shallowed, her heartbeat speeded up; that same old devil – fight-or-flight – she'd battled with for years. She'd always felt particularly cautious in groups, but everyone here seemed pleasant enough. Why are you being such an old fool? she asked herself. There's no bully taking up all the space, at least not yet. Judy's real worry was that she'd say something stupid; Greta was the clever one, the academic. Perhaps I should have said yes to that glass of wine after all, she thought.

'*The Haunting of Hill House.*' Freya began, 'written by our club's namesake, Shirley Jackson. First published in 1959. It's said she got her inspiration from an article about real life psychic researchers in the 19th Century. What interested her was not so much the haunting, but the personalities of the researchers themselves. It's a classic haunted house story, arguably the best one ever written. A Dr Montague leads the investigation into psychic phenomena at the notorious Hill House. With him are Luke, the young man set to inherit the house, and two young women, Eleanor and Theodora, both of whom have been chosen because they are 'sensitives', people with extrasensory abilities. Of those two women, the main character, Eleanor, is the most in tune with the supernatural forces at work in the house, perhaps because she's also the most deeply troubled of all the characters. As the story progresses, horrifying things start happening to her.' Freya paused momentarily. 'So gang, what do we all think?'

Nancy crossed one leg over the other, 'The house is the fifth presence in the story – or the first. Its windows are described as watching eyes. It gives you that horrible feeling – that someone is looking at you without your wanting it or giving permission.'

'The layout of the house is cleverly used,' Sebastian said. 'Everything's out of alignment. It's a higgledy-piggledy jumbled up place. And people keep getting lost between rooms.'

'And there are the windowless rooms, and the doors that keep closing,' Nancy said.

'What about Eleanor, the main character?' Freya asked.

'She's lonely,' Preet said, 'and the house latches on to

her because of that. It finds her vulnerability and her pain. And, is no one else getting the lesbian vibe between Eleanor and Theodora? Theodora has a roommate, whose gender is never specified, who she had a quarrel with before coming to the house. Eleanor and Theodora are so tactile and intimate, even down to wearing each other's clothes. It's all there.'

'And Theodora calls Eleanor 'Nell',' Nancy nodded in agreement, 'which is either a pet name or something more mocking.'

'The jumbled-up-ness of the house echoes the confused lives of the characters,' Sebastian said, bringing the discussion back to his earlier point. 'It's a mixed up place, a confused mess, like most people's minds.'

'I like the idea of dislocation – houses, people, minds,' Freya said. 'And the lesbianism: there's a definite ambivalence when Theodora calls Eleanor 'Nell' like she's an impressionable child not to be taken entirely seriously.'

'What about you, Judy?' Freya said.

Everyone turned to look at Judy. Her palms were damp, her mouth suddenly dry. 'I didn't really see the lesbian side of things,' she said, her voice breaking a little.

Silence. Stretching out. Seemingly interminably.

Silence.

'I'm not really big on horror,' she managed to get out, 'so I found the whole thing rather disconcerting.'

Silence again.

Empty air.

Good God! She felt like she was at a job interview. 'I suppose,' she said, 'I felt rather sorry for Eleanor. She seems so very lonely. We all are in one way or another, though, aren't we? You can only experience your own humanity directly, in a solitary way, can't you? No one else can be inside your head with you.'

'I think you've hit the nail!' Freya said. 'At the end Eleanor drives her car at speed into a tree and kills herself – an absolutely stellar ending to a novel. Then the book ends with that line about the consciousness that remains inside Hill House: 'whatever walked there walked alone'. Is that Eleanor's ghost and the ghosts of other lonely and isolated women? Is Eleanor Everyman, or Everywoman?'

Judy felt cautiously pleased with herself. Not quite so incapable after all. Not such a Miss Mouse. Just maybe she was having one of Abraham Maslow's peak experiences here in the basement of this odd little bookshop, talking about a horror story of all things.

'And what about the last paragraph,' Freya asked, 'when Montague publishes his findings on supernatural occurrences at Hill House, and the academic community completely ignores him?'

'That's Shirley Jackson taking a swipe at the literary world,' said Preet. 'No one really takes the horror genre seriously. No one sees it as literature.'

'Cocking a snook at them all!' Judy said, rather louder than she intended.

V

'Oh, do come next week. Promise you will,' Freya said.

'I'm not really a horror buff,' Judy replied. '*Hill House* is only the second horror novel I've ever read.'

'What was the first?'

'*The Castle of Otranto*. A very long time ago.'

'What an absolute belter! Do say you'll come back next

33

week. My reasons are not entirely unselfish.' Freya pulled the door to Persephone's closed for the night. 'I like having a woman of my own generation in the group. And I'm sure you'll enjoy the next book. Toni Morrison is superb and *Beloved* is beautifully written, albeit about a harrowing topic. And it's much shorter than *It*.'

'*It*?'

'Stephen King. Our last book. Over a thousand pages long. I had to allow everybody a bit more time to get through it. Controversial but expertly put together like all King's work. Sebastian was fascinated by the killer clown, Pennywise. He said he'd put something similar in his next book, cheeky old devil.' Freya unchained her bicycle. 'Are you on foot?'

'Yes, I'm only in the Kite, Eden Street.'

'I'm on Ferry Path, just over the river.' Freya nudged Judy's arm. 'Say you'll come next week.'

vi

Mist rubbed its back along Eden Street. The little hallway seemed darker than usual. Judy was still thinking about Eleanor. What a lonely character she was. Eleanor's sense of separateness was a little too close for comfort. 94 Eden Street felt cold and empty ever since... even more so with the tug of autumn in the air. She'd thought of moving but too much life had been lived here; it was home to too many good memories. She sat up in bed with a cup of cocoa and *Novel on Yellow Paper*. A draft whispered in through a gap in the casement; she needed to find a man to repair the rotten sill. She shivered slightly and put down the book; she couldn't concentrate tonight. She hadn't met anyone new in almost a year, not since... Most of the people she called her friends had been Greta's workmates from the university; professors of this, doctors of that. Now, with Greta gone, she rarely saw any of them except in passing; entirely her own fault. She'd been invited to a dinner party here, drinks and nibbles there, but she couldn't summon up the mettle to face them on her own, particularly at some rarified social gathering: 'Poor old Judy, she was Greta Sanderson's wife. Very seasoned academic, Greta, credit to the college. Terrible shame.' Judy was the 'little woman', the domestic backbone behind the great professor. And so she had become the involuntary custodian of the life they used to live together; the books, the academic papers, Greta's old clothes and classical records; everything still in its place in the unrelenting silence. But tonight at the book group had been all right, better than she'd expected, and she'd got through it. That felt important: hurdles and milestones and all that.

She liked Freya, her indomitability, the sparkle in her soft brown eyes. Sebastian was likeable enough in an old-school kind of way. The young women had the self-assurance so typical of Cambridge students. And she knew only too well, from her years with Greta, that the university worked them extremely hard. Plenty of Saturday nights spent wading through reams of literary criticism or working on assignments from their supervisors. Not really the life that young people should be living, Judy thought. She found herself warming to the idea of going back to the group next week. She realised, with the faintest hint of a smile, that she could rather get used to the Shirley Jackson Club.

The telephone rang.

It was Freya. 'Sorry for calling so late. I haven't woken you, have I? Sebastian has asked me to collect an antique mirror for him, and a rare first edition. A Shirley Jackson no less! But they're in London and the dear old thing would prefer not to hike all the way into town.'

'Can't he have them delivered?'

'Doesn't trust the post. Lost a manuscript back in '71. The only copy. I was thinking of going the day after tomorrow. Would you keep me company? We could have some lunch, make a day of it.'

Judy paused: Freya Bancroft, middle-aged bookshop owner, untamed bohemian, New Age law-unto-herself. Judy bit her lower lip – this could all get a little out of hand.

'All right,' she said, 'why not!'

chapter two

"Their throats will burn when the words come out,
and in their bellies they will feel a torment hotter
than a thousand fires."
WE HAVE ALWAYS LIVED IN THE CASTLE | SHIRLEY JACKSON

*No sunlight reached Bantock's
Fine Antiques and Collectibles.*

i

Autumn sunshine fingered its way uncertainly between The City's high-rise towers. None of its warming light found Bantock's Fine Antiques and Collectibles, hidden in a nondescript passageway choked with shadow. Judy was reminded of Bill Sykes and Daniel Quilp – and the dread of reading aloud in front of the class. She was a capable student but never had much confidence in her own opinion. 'You're an honest plodder, Judy Miller,' was her form mistress's assessment. Praise indeed!

The sharp ring of the brass bell startled her. The sulky interior was musty with age and a little decay. Heavy oak chests, gilded coffers, worn tapestries, corroded bronze statues oxidised to an oily, dirty brown; nothing warm or inviting here. It was like a fire sale in a gothic mansion. The two women negotiated an obstacle course of chimeras and grotesques. At the back of the shop, beaded curtains swished firmly aside like coy Victorian petticoats and a small, thin man said, 'Good morning, ladies.' Crabby lines danced at the corners of his mouth; the rest of his face was similarly grizzled, and aquiline; grey hair was thrust haphazardly upwards by a green eyeshade and his grey felt waistcoat was shiny and faded with age. Clapped out, thought Judy

'What can I do for you?' The man's stare put Judy on her guard.

'We've come to collect two items for Mr Sebastian Sizemore,' Freya said. 'I believe he telephoned you?'

Without taking his eyes off Freya and Judy, the man lifted an ornate oval mirror onto the counter top: faded glass, a little blown, as if wispy clouds were trapped inside; snarling gargoyles and lustreless gold leaves around the frame; about thirty inches high in all. Some of the gargoyles were crouching, ready to pounce; others were flying, circling for prey. Judy thought the whole thing repugnant. Freya seemed delighted. She ran her fingers lovingly around the gilt frame as if admiring the lines of a classic sports car.

'And the book?' Freya asked. The shopkeeper's gaze remained fixed on her as he produced a hardback copy of *We Have Always Lived in the Castle* by Shirley Jackson. The title on the dust jacket was written in an uneven, undulating script, as was the author's name. Underneath was a pencil drawing of a black cat sitting in long grass. The cat's head was an oddity; it had no mouth or nose and its eyes were drawn as elongated black pupils in narrow white slits. Its head was darker than the rest of its body, giving it the air of a 19th-century executioner – or a rapist in a balaclava. Judy couldn't see how the book's cover would encourage anyone to buy it.

'This is the original cover,' Freya said reverentially, opening the book carefully. Inside was a publisher's slip: a beautifully drawn longship printed on thick cream paper denoted the Viking Press. A rectangle of dots and diamonds contained the publisher's address, title, author, and price of $3.95. First publication date was given as 21st of September 1962 accompanied by the words *Advanced Reading Copy*. This was a review copy. On the title page, in wavy black ink, was the book's singular glory: the signature of Shirley Jackson herself.

'How did you acquire these items?' Freya was full of wonder and enthusiasm, hallmarks of the unabashed fan.

'Through a contact at Wolfbane Books, the publishing house,' the man said. 'They acquired both items some years ago. They were held in their vault with a number of other rarities.' He wrapped the mirror and the book in sheets of tissue paper before gently easing them into a bag.

Judy was glad to get out into the daylight and the bustle of London's lively streets. There was something blighted about Bantock's Fine Antiques and Collectibles. She hoped she never had to go there again.

ii

Just another afternoon at Brasserie Zedel. Waiters strode confidently across the brightly lit room in black and white uniforms, trays of champagne flutes and brightly coloured cocktails held high. Zedel was once the breakfast room of the Regent Palace Hotel, a glorious art deco salon in a cavernous basement just off Piccadilly. Below the monumental Zedel clock, two women were having lunch, oblivious to the surrounding hubbub.

'He paid how much?!' Judy almost dropped her bread in the French onion soup.

'Two thousand pounds,' Freya repeated earnestly. 'That was just for the book. The mirror came in at much less. Twelve hundred, I think.'

'Good God!'

'The mirror is from Shirley Jackson's house on Main Street in Bennington. Can you imagine? Jackson looking into that mirror, her reflection looking back.'

'It seems rather steep to me,' Judy said dubiously. She remembered Greta paying more than five hundred pounds for Gertrude Stein's *Lucy Church Amiably* in the Plain Edition and that was back in 1993. Horror must be really big business.

'A Shirley Jackson first edition is rare as gold dust to a horror fan,' Freya said. 'Once you get into it, horror is terribly moreish, like a box of Belgian truffles. It's not the most respected of genres, and that gives it a certain illicit quality, like a lover your parents don't approve of. To err is human but it feels divine!'

It would be a while before Judy was convinced. 'That reminds me,' she said, 'I need to pick up a copy of *Beloved* for next week.'

'We'll drop into one of the secondhand booksellers on Charing Cross Road on our way home,' Freya said. 'See if we can't get you a first edition. You can show it off to the group.'

'As long as it's not two thousand pounds.'

Freya laughed.

'Tell me about this book: *We Have Always Lived in the Castle,*' Judy said.

Freya leaned forwards excitedly. 'Three surviving members of a reclusive family live in an isolated mansion on the edge of a village. And one of them is a poisoner. It was Jackson's last novel and is considered to be her finest. It was published in 1962, just three years before she died. It's essentially about being an outsider,' here Freya paused knowingly, 'and about the suspicion directed towards outsiders.'

'Is it on the reading list for the group or have you done it already?'

'Not yet, but we'll read and discuss all Jackson's books eventually.'

'I'm looking forward to that one.'

Freya was a schoolgirl all of a sudden on the last day of term, brimming with ideas of the fun to be had with her new best friend. 'You're staying with the group, then?'

'Yes,' Judy said. 'I think I'll stick with it. If you'll have me?'

'And,' Freya hesitated, 'in the interests of getting to know you better. What happened to your wife? Sebastian wasn't the only one who noticed the two of you on your walks around Cambridge.'

Judy rested her spoon slowly and deliberately on her plate. She liked Freya; she was plucky and cheerful and she'd certainly made Judy welcome at the book club. 'Greta died last year,' Judy said. 'Since then I've been a bit of a recluse.'

Freya took Judy's hand in hers. 'That's perfectly understandable,' she said. Her smile was warm and watchful. It made Judy feel as if she were being welcomed home from a long journey. She hadn't been very willing, or able, to talk about Greta. It had been difficult to bring the pain out into the light and confront it. Her life had lost its poetry – all their easy routines like scouring the flyers on the railings around All Saints Garden to discover a talk about Stein or Woolf or Cather; a lazy summer's afternoon strolling along the Backs; all these simple pleasures were impossible now. But Freya made things different and easier somehow. Time with Freya opened a door, gave Judy a glimpse of a possible future. Freya offered a moment in the sunshine where, however momentarily, Judy could overcome her feeling of long-drawn-out defeat.

'How long were you together?' Freya asked. 'Ever since I arrived in Cambridge, you were both a bit of a fixture in town.'

'Greta lectured in Greek and Roman history,' Judy said. It surprised her how good it was to talk about Greta, and how much she felt she could trust Freya. 'We moved to Cambridge in '92, not long after we met.'

'What about you? Did you work at the university?'

'No, I thought about getting some sort of secretarial job but there was enough to do running our lives at home. So I became the professional homemaker.'

'Behind every great woman... there has to be a great woman?'

'Perhaps.' Judy smiled.

'The stay-at-home role is often undervalued. And now you feel a bit rudderless?'

The comment was well-meant, but it landed like a punch in the gut.

'I suppose I do. Greta was a bit of a workaholic, always with her head in a book, or marking a pile of essays. But it's not really work if you love your subject. Most of the friends we had were colleagues of Greta's from the faculty or elsewhere in the university.'

'Do you know George and Martha? He's a professor of history. She's a piece of work. They're both Americans. I've sold them a good few books over the years, ancient cultures and traditions, very specialist stuff. I often have to order in. He's one of my best customers, though, willing to pay well for a rare edition. They've been at Cambridge for absolutely ages. Their drinking and their rows are the stuff of legend.'

'I know George and Martha all right,' Judy said. 'When they've had a skinful, it's not much fun – except for them perhaps – and definitely time to go home.' She suddenly had a strong desire to change the subject. 'Tell me about you.'

'Much like your late wife, I'm a bit of a workaholic. And I also love what I do. When I came out of university, clutching my English Literature degree, I worked at Foyles in Charing Cross Road. I've always been interested in alternative spiritualities, as they call them now, particularly neopaganism. I eventually landed a job at Treadwell's when they first opened in Covent Garden but, after a while, the thing I wanted most was to run my own shop. I started an esoteric bookshop in Clerkenwell with another witch. When she moved to Brighton in 2016, I decided it was time for a change too so I hopped on my broomstick, landed in Cambridge, and set up Persephone's.'

'I don't know much about neopaganism at all,' Judy said

shyly.

'We don't sacrifice goats or eat small babies.'

'I didn't think —.'

'We might do a little semi-naked dancing in the woods, though.' Freya winked. Judy laughed out loud; she couldn't recall when she'd last laughed.

'Can I have a look at that very rare and expensive book again?' she asked. According to the back cover, Edmund Fuller of *The New York Times* described Shirley Jackson as 'the finest master currently practicing in the genre of the cryptic, haunted tale.' *The Boston Herald* said she could 'install eeriness and suspense with a superlatively artful hand' and *The Pittsburgh Press* wrote that the book's 'tightrope balance between fantasy and terrible reality' made it a 'technical marvel'.

'For a genre that's not particularly well respected, this book has some good reviews,' Judy said.

Freya prodded her goat's cheese salad. 'You can always rely on a woman to do a job properly,' she said, 'specially if she also happens to be a witch.'

'Shirley Jackson was a witch?'

iii

Chesterton Hall Crescent. A parabola of bay windows, tall chimneys, well-tended front gardens with lovely masses of lilacs, lavenders and trailing ivy. Sebastian Sizemore's villa stood out from the rest; a little further back from the road, more than a little unkempt; its overgrown bushes hanging over the pavement; tatty rattan garden furniture under windows parched for want of a lick of paint. The dinner party set sniped and griped about the old horror writer 'lowering the tone' of *The Crescent* but, as is the way with these things, no one uttered a word to the man himself.

Carefully, Sebastian wiped dust from the glass of Shirley Jackson's mirror. The damp of the basement was masked by the smell of hot wax and a little smoke from the guttering candles. The unreliable flames sent shadows skittering into the corners of the room and lit the faces of the mirror's snarling gargoyles. There was a bitter taste in the air; perfect for communing with the dead. It put Sebastian in mind of his book, *The Devil's Maidens*: convent school girls summon up Lucifer as part of a Halloween prank then, one by one, each of them comes to a nasty end. Alicia Brightwell, his busty-blonde heroine, is the sole survivor or 'final girl' as they called it nowadays. He liked Alicia. He brought her back for the sequel, *The Devil's Mistress*, set in London this time rather than Dorset with Alicia now the wife of Joshua van Horne, a wealthy stockbroker (and Satanist). Joshua married Alicia not for love but for the *Mark of Lucifer* she bore on her left breast from her earlier Satanic encounter. That scar marked her out as the next great sacrifice to the Lord of Darkness.

Sebastian started work on the book back in 1976. He spent that long, burning summer sitting in front of his Olivetti Lettera 31.

Blocked.

Totally out of the blue, the nightmare of writer's block hit him like a speeding truck. One day he was writing free, flowing prose, the next: bang!

He hit the buffers – a creative dead end.

He sought help from his old friend, Johnnie Walker,

hoping this would loosen him up, unchain his paralysed imagination but it didn't work. In the end he drank, not to write, but to stem the tide of panic and despair.

He needed the money badly then and needed it now. Years of high living had emptied his bank account. Like a child blowing a dandelion clock, he'd huffed and puffed away his advances and royalties and they vanished on the wind. Liquid lunches with Leslie Charteris. Evenings at The Garrick Club with Dennis Wheatley; the unforgettable dinner in November '64, Wheatley celebrating the release of *They Used Dark Forces*. Hugh Astor, Joseph Gluckstein Links and the Duke of Richmond; the guest list was a roll call of the rich, famous, and privileged. At the end of the night, Sebastian stumbled into a chauffeur-driven Silver Cloud, Wheatley's son Anthony beside him, sniping drunkenly about his wicked stepmother. Those were the good old days. Sebastian was a bold young writer then with a couple of bestsellers under his belt; although he knew he was still a little wet behind the ears, still learning the craft, a neophyte at the feet of the masters.

Maybe all that wine and whisky had addled his brain. Somehow he'd crawled his way to the final chapter of *The Devil's Mistress*, to the final showdown in the ruins of a haunted castle. When the novel finally hit the bookshops in the summer of 1978, it was panned by the critics. Truth be told, they'd panned most of his titles – hateful bastards, wannabe novelists – but this time it was different, the critics had been particularly bloodthirsty: 'Childish nonsense about a bird-brained heroine whose character is paper thin' wrote the *New York Times*; 'Hammer studios' days are numbered, and so it seems are those of Mr S.J.

Sizemore. Do we really need more of his puerile nonsense in print?' asked *The Manchester Guardian*. *The TLS*, unsurprisingly, didn't mention *The Devil's Mistress* at all. The book failed to fly off the shelves and Pan dropped him. Nobody else seemed interested in an author who was thought out of date or, as *The Telegraph* put it, 'the very definition of passé'.

Nowadays it was different. Now there were Facebook fan pages. Instagram accounts labelled *@sizemoresuperfan* or *@brightwellbabe*. First editions sold for hundreds of pounds on eBay according to the youngsters at the Shirley Jackson Club. They spurred him on, asked when he was going to come out of retirement and write another *great horror novel*. He'd thought about it often enough. He'd given it a try now and again. He'd scribbled down a few ideas, even got as far as a cockeyed synopsis.

Then Block.

Every year the great big comeback mountain looked higher, rockier, more insurmountable. Now he was really afraid he'd never write again.

Blocked.

Hours spent watching the cursor flash against his hopelessly blank Word document. He started 'googling' himself; grew rather addicted to that. He searched for his books on the web to see the fan chatter and to find out exactly how much a signed copy of *The Devil's Maidens* was going for these days. He didn't know why he'd suddenly thought of Shirley Jackson, searched her name, found little bits and bobs of memorabilia for sale. He certainly didn't know why he'd bought the mirror – on impulse perhaps, a throwback to the good old days; the young and reckless writer splashing the cash.

The mirror transported him there – to Main Street, North Bennington, to Shirley Jackson's house, the house of the writer, housewife and witch. He closed his eyes, reached out and touch the misted surface of the glass; he could see the yellow paper piled up next to her typewriter; he could hear her sing-song voice:

> *'The first was young Miss Grattan*
> *She tried not to let him in,*
> *He stabbed her with a corn knife*
> *That's how his crimes begin.'*

And, there and then, he realised there was no point looking to the present: Instagram, Tik Tok, fan groups; all that malarkey. What he needed was a window onto the past.

Hurrying to the attic, he brushed the dust off his old Olivetti, poured himself a glass of Cognac, raised it in a silent toast to absent friends, to teachers and masters, to Dennis, to Leslie, to Ronald Chetwynd-Hayes, even those clever little whippersnappers Barker and King, and wrote the perfect sentence, the perfect opening, and he knew whence the gift had come: Ms. Shirley Jackson.

Now he needs more inspiration, more help from his new teacher. He sits in the dim basement, walls flowered with damp, faithful old Olivetti and Shirley Jackson first edition at his side. Candles burn in an unsteady circle around the edges of the room. The mirror hangs from a rusty nail. Fingers of shadow touch and withdraw from the old author's face. Like most fans of the genre, he knows Jackson dabbled in the unknown. He also realises, instinctively, that some part of her has been reaching out to him. Now he needs her to reach out again. He laces his fingers together as if in supplication. He senses everything keenly now; the wettish odour in the air; cunning little creaks from the floorboards above; his own long sigh; he has been unconsciously holding his breath. Then he whispers into the encroaching dark.

'Shirley Hardie Jackson… Shirley Hardie Jackson… Shirley Hardie Jackson…'

Silence.

Cool, stony silence as if from something that watches and waits.

He repeats the words, holding his voice steady: 'I summon you now, Shirley Hardie Jackson… Shirley Hardie Jackson… Shirley Hardie Jackson…'

Still nothing.

Nothing disturbs the watching waiting silence.

He places his hands behind his head and stretches; a bone in his neck clicks. He feels tired, cold and old, and so bloody useless. What was he thinking? He is a stupid old man, a silly old bugger, acting out a scene from some hackneyed horror novel; something you'd find in an 'out-of-date' S.J. Sizemore mass-market potboiler.

He cups his palms and blows into them to combat the cold.

And there it is: the faintest whistling, like wind gusting down a chimney. There, in the waiting silence. There it is again. He looks into the mirror. Condensation is forming on the glass. He watches it advance until it obscures the whole surface. He moves closer. Something is forming in the middle of the glass. Drops of condensation run together, like blood from a wound, forming the word, YES.

chapter three

"I waited for you
 You are mine
 You are mine
 You are mine"
BELOVED | TONI MORRISON

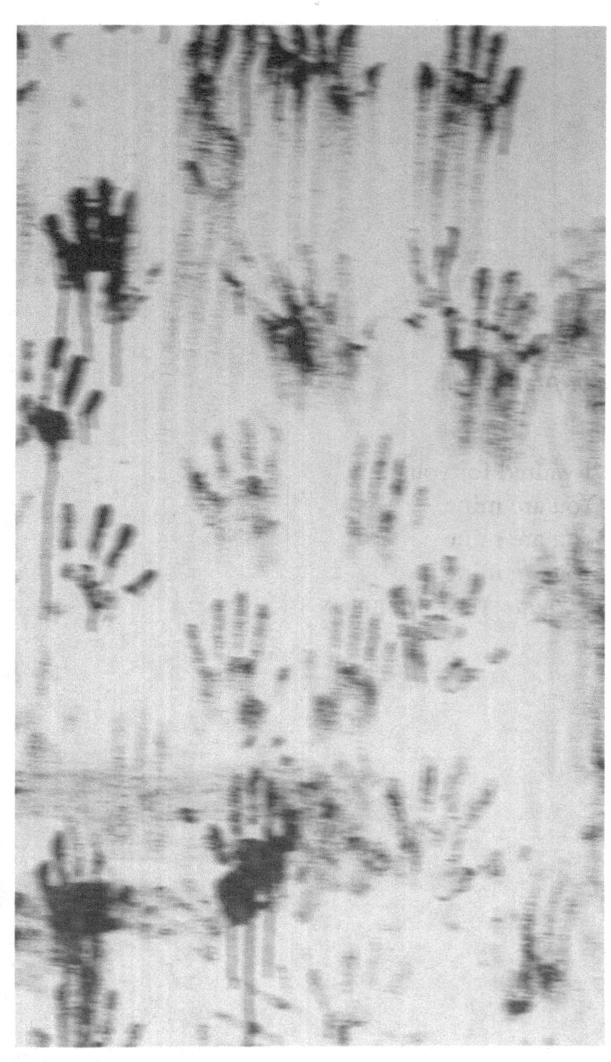

*Small handprints form on the misty surface of the glass
like a child's hands pressing into clay.*

i

Preet's MacBook Air rests on the kitchen worktop; behind it, a notice tacked to the red-and-white tiles: *all electrical items are to be switched off when not in use.* Preet, Nancy and two young men are sitting at a dining table battle-scarred by years of misuse: student parties, drinking games, celebration or commiseration dinners. Beside the laptop a disc drive buzzes like a fly. The students' faces are wraith-like in the greenish glow from the screen. Horror night is a weekly ritual; a chance to switch off from course work, responsibility and reading lists for two precious hours.

A baronial hall in a brooding gothic castle, a place long forsaken by God and by man. Heraldic flags, a faded tapestry, a monumental sixteen-arm silver candelabrum on a heavy oak sideboard. Half-light speaks of the fast-approaching dawn. Christopher Lee's Dracula races up wide stone stairs, his cloak rippling behind him like dark wings.

Peter Cushing's Van Helsing follows in determined pursuit: he must destroy the monster who has terrorised so many through the ages. Pulsing violins underline the urgency of Van Helsing's attempt to dispatch the vampire. Dracula hurries across the chequered marble floor, past a great terrestrial globe set on a wooden tripod, and here Van Helsing corners him. Here they fall together in mortal combat. The vampire count's fingers close around Van Helsing's throat and, try as he might, Van Helsing cannot release the terrible death grip. Now Dracula bows towards his adversary like a tender lover; his lips part, baring the teeth that will pierce Van Helsing's flesh.

Van Helsing's eyes snap open. Summoning the last of his strength, he manages to throw Dracula off, backing away as the count advances. Now the doctor's mind is racing: how to defeat the monstrous creature? In one final, frantic bid, he climbs onto the banqueting table, leaps at the windows and tears down the curtains allowing shafts of early morning sunlight to enter the room and strike the undead horror.

Van Helsing takes up two candlesticks, forming a makeshift cross, and brandishes it at the count. Hissing and writhing in agony, the vampire begins to wither; the camera switches back and forth between hero and monster, hero and monster, hero and monster. Dracula's body decays with astonishing rapidity, agitated ever so gently by a breeze from the window until it has crumbled entirely to dust.

The soundtrack builds to a crescendo now; the camera closes in on Count Dracula's golden signet ring, the only surviving evidence of the vampire's existence and a signal, perhaps, that the evil will inevitably return. The end credits roll in distinctive gothic lettering the colour of blood.

'I bloody love a good old Hammer horror,' Nancy said looking around at the others.

'Same here,' said Preet, taking a tortilla chip from a bowl in the centre of the table and waving it towards the screen. 'Is *Dracula* the first ever horror film Hammer made?'

Tom has all the answers as usual: 'That honour goes to *The Curse of Frankenstein*,' he said in his keen, Irish lilt, 'which came out in 1957. Unless, that is, you count *Quatermass* as a horror movie, which I don't.' His violet eyes were startling behind round, wire-rimmed glasses. He wasn't handsome in the usual way, but he was not easily forgotten, either.

'The ending of this film is pretty famous?' Leon was as dark as Tom was fair, of Caribbean heritage, unashamedly good-looking with thick hair cut short in a twisted hightop.

'People say it's the best finale of any of the Dracula films, at least the Christopher Lee ones.'

'I thought the Gary Oldman movie was better,' said Preet. 'Scarier because the effects were more convincing.'

'But this one's pretty good for it's time,' said Leon. 'They did a bang-up job with what they had.'

'Which wasn't much,' said Nancy, taking off her glasses and wiping them furiously with a paper napkin. 'Jeepers, these glasses are filthy dirty.'

'Believe it or not,' Tom said, 'some of it was considered too shocking for people at the time. There were extra shots of Dracula disintegrating, and one of him pulling the flesh away from his own face. All cut out. They were discovered years later in a vault in Japan.'

Nancy grinned. 'Nothing scares us Japanese.'

'Except *Zombie Flesh Eaters* a few weeks ago,' Preet pointed out uncharitably.

'I can't stand zombies. Isn't there a zombie novel coming up for the Shirley club?'

'Yes. *I am Legend*. There's a film of that too, isn't there?' Preet looked at Tom.

'Three in fact!' Tom sounded rather pleased with himself. 'The first was *The Last Man on Earth* made in the 1960s with Vincent Price, black and white. Then they filmed it in colour as *The Omega Man* in the 1970s with Charlton Heston. The most recent version was with Will Smith. Strictly speaking, the monsters in *I Am Legend* are vampires, not zombies.'

'My brother dragged me along to see the Will Smith,' Nancy said. 'It was nasty. The zombies or vampires, or whatever they were, wanting the flesh off your bones. Freaked me out.'

'You could have just concentrated on Will Smith. He was really hot back then,' Tom said. 'Much sexier than Charlton Heston.'

'Wasn't he just?' said Leon, winking at Tom. 'But *The Omega Man* had the interracial kiss between Charlton Heston and Rosalind Cash. Brave for the time. Especially in America.' He yawned and stretched his arms out theatrically. 'I'm going to hit the sack. I've got a ton of supervision work to do tomorrow. Good old Jane Austen.'

It wasn't very long before Tom pushed back his chair purposefully. 'I think I'll turn in as well.'

Nancy and Preet traded knowing glances.

Staircase five seemed especially dark. Leon rarely put the light on; he preferred the dark; more atmospheric. He imagined vampires, werewolves, knife-wielding maniacs leaping out from the dark and enjoyed the sharp little thrill of fear it gave him; as if he were the star of his own horror film. The feeling of danger, his fate hanging by a thread, was something to keep the senses awake in an otherwise numbing world of essays and lectures and bland microwaveable food.

But this time, staircase five seemed especially dark.

Leon had never been allowed to watch horror movies as a child. They were forbidden fruit, like kissing other boys. He'd tasted that particular fruit the first chance he got: a secret embrace in a deserted high school changing room. All the other boys had gone home. There was the usual horseplay, whipping buttocks and legs with wet towels, chasing each other round the room. Leon slipped on the wet floor and Amani Williams (short dreadlocks; soft brown eyes) picked him up, studied his face for a moment, then their lips touched, then they were exploring each other with trembling fingers; kissing, masturbating. Time alone together became an illicit addiction, a reason for living. Then, just like that, Amani was gone. It was as if he had ceased to exist. No one wanted to talk about him. Leon discovered much later that Amani's mother had taken an overdose. He had been spirited away to another place, another city – no one knew quite where – to live with an uncle. Leon filled the emptiness with study, with books. The emptiness was still there but his grades improved; so much so that his form tutor suggested he try for Oxbridge. Now here he was, the poor boy from

Jamaica, one of the privileged few amongst the dreaming spires of Cambridge.

He turned the key in the lock (why was it always so stiff?) and flicked on the anglepoise lamp beside the single bed. The sheets were rumpled. He should change them, put a wash on.

He paused, head at a tilt, registering an unfamiliar scraping sound: outside his bedroom window a fat red balloon was rubbing against the glass in angry little jerks like a fly caught in a web. There was something written on the balloon. He moved closer but couldn't make out what it said. He touched the glass and snatched his hand back, stung; the window was ferociously cold and a small crack had suddenly appeared. He stared, fascinated, as the balloon continued its insane twitching and thrashing and the crack crept further and further across the glass. A sharp knock at the door distracted him. When he turned back to the window, the balloon was gone.

Tom was waiting expectantly in the hallway, hands in pockets. Leon grabbed him by the collar and pulled him inside. Tom nudged the door shut behind him with the heel of his boot as Leon pulled him towards the bed.

They undress. They lie down on the floor, senses inflamed by their sweet scrutiny of each other, kissing skin, eyelids, arms, nipples. They turn, head to tail, their lips taking in the urgent length of the other, fingers cupping balls in unison with elegantly judged pressure. Tenderly, the moment comes, a burst of warmth at the back of the throat then they climb into the little single bed, a tangle of tired limbs and sleepy heads and drift into oblivion until morning.

Shirley Jackson Club Meeting:
Beloved – Toni Morrison.

The wrinkles on her cheeks and around her eyes gave her a thoughtful air; all in all, it was a solid and dependable kind of face. Leon observed Judy Miller from across the room and decided he liked the club's newest member. She reminded him in some ways of Tashelle, his mother's older sister. Aunt Tashelle lived most of her life in the same small block of flats in Tottenham. She was small and slim, much smaller than Leon's mother. She saw life for what it was and forgave it all its imperfections. Leon had often stayed in her roomy flat in the school holidays, watching closely as she prepared ackee and saltfish. She always used tinned ackee and bell peppers that were different colours 'to make the dish look like a rainbow after rain'. She bought the saltfish on the bone; said it held its flavour better that way. And she insisted on fresh thyme: 'Everything going into your body should be succulent and fresh, no point in using no dried up flakes of anything – it's bad for the soul.' Leon was too polite to point out that tinned ackee wasn't fresh. Once she'd removed the bone and skin from the saltfish and crumbled the flesh between her fingers, she'd fry onions, tomatoes, peppers and chillies, busy hands flitting over the pan as she added each ingredient. She let everything soften together a while: 'This is where the real magic starts,' she'd tell him as the ingredients crackled and sizzled. 'Can you hear them singing to each other now?' When not laughing her distinctive ringing laugh, Tashelle spoke softly, giving the impression she found the everyday business of life just a little bit amusing. The mischief of the world could never get under her skin.

Finally she'd add the flaked saltfish and the ackee, careful not to stir too hard. 'You don't want any mushiness,' she'd say, handing him the wooden spoon and gently nudging his cheek. Aunt Tashelle was warmth and love and acceptance mounded up and made into a woman; always ready to encourage him in every new bright idea his childish mind conjured up. When he told her he wanted to be an astronaut: 'Brilliant idea, lovely – we need to explore what's out there beyond the sky.' When he decided to be a singer: 'Wonderful, darling, people always want to hear a lovely song.' And when he decided to go to Cambridge and study English, with a hope of becoming a writer: 'Perfect, my angel – you've got lots of magical stories inside you just waiting to be told.' To Aunt Tashelle every day was another step forward in the adventure of life. She never told him his ideas were pie in the sky or that he needed something to fall back on, a proper career. She was the first person he came out to. She hugged him hard: 'You must follow your heart, darling. No use in pretending to be someone you're not just to please other folks.' When Tashelle died, (peacefully, smiling in her sleep, of course), his mother handed him a battered old exercise book. It was full of his aunt's favourite recipes, the first ones scribbled down when she was no more than sixteen.

'She wanted you to have this,' his mother told him. Now, whenever he wanted to make a special meal for Tom, or his friends on staircase five, he'd go straight to aunt Tashelle's battered old notebook; 'my little book of tricks' she always called it. Leon wondered idly if Judy had a nephew or a niece; whether she handed down her own favourite recipes, or favourite books or whatever it was that defined her.

Judy looked down at the copy of *Beloved* in her lap. 'It's an incredibly powerful book,' she said, 'one of the most powerful books I've ever read. Such beautiful writing about something so horrific.'

Nancy nodded slowly. 'Slavery's the real monster. The awful tragedy of a woman killing her child to save it from a life of slavery.'

'And when the ghost of the child comes back,' Freya said, 'it's full of anger, of course, and the ferocity of that rage creates a terrible psychic disturbance: things move in the house, furniture is broken. Eventually the dead child returns completely in the physical body of a young woman.'

'I think it shows that the idea of being 'free' after emancipation is a lie,' Leon said. 'The degradation of slavery lives on in the trauma it leaves behind. It's a terrible legacy and it destroys people mentally and physically. That trauma stays with all former slaves for the rest of their lives. How could it not?'

'I think the main character, Sethe, symbolises a very particular struggle for women in slavery,' said Nancy, 'the awful fact that their children will be born slaves. She is haunted by the idea that the only way out is infanticide.'

'It was inspired by a true story,' said Preet, 'about a woman called Margaret Garner.'

'Everyone I know who's read *Beloved*,' said Freya, 'has been incredibly moved by it. After reading it, you're not quite the same person.'

'You come to understand the scars of slavery left on whole communities, and how that scarring carries over from generation to generation,' said Leon. 'That's the power in what Toni Morrison is saying, I think.'

'And Sethe's house, 124 Bluestone Road, is another creepy and nightmarish house,' said Freya. 'Much like Shirley Jackson's Hill House. And, of course, number 55 Lodovico Street.'

Judy looked puzzled.

'It's the setting for *The Hellbound Heart*,' Freya said. 'We read Clive Barker a while back, before you joined.'

'*Beloved* has elements of gothic horror,' Tom said, 'but it seems, to me, to lean towards magical realism, like an Angela Carter.'

'Don't get me started on the genius of Angela Carter.' Freya winked at him.

Tom laughed.

'I think you've got a point,' Freya said. 'It *is* Carteresque in places, particularly in the character of *Beloved* – she's essentially a ghost of flesh and blood. The truly supernatural elements are mostly at the beginning of the book, when the ghost of *Beloved* hasn't yet taken solid form, when she's breaking things in the house and causing the house to shake.'

'And making her handprints appear on the cake,' said Tom.

'Yes, in those passages.'

'The white characters are not all one-dimensional, either, not all evil or unsympathetic,' said Leon. 'There's some balance and some compassion in the characterisation. The poverty-stricken white girl who helps Sethe deliver her baby.'

'The violence and torture are almost too much to read,' said Preet. 'You really have to steel yourself. One of the darkest times in human history.'

'A beautiful read,' Freya said, 'and a terrifying one.'

iv

Freya rubbed one eye wearily with the heel of her hand. The discussion of *Beloved* had run way over time, which was wonderful but a little exhausting too. It was almost half past nine as she cycled onto Ferry Path. Darkness pooled between the street lamps and a mist was curling up from the river. She rang Sebastian as soon as she got home. It wasn't like him to miss a meeting, especially without telling her first. There was no answer so she left a voicemail; she hoped he was all right. Funny old stick, she thought, old-fashioned and a little out of place in the modern world. But maybe, so am I, she thought. She smiled to herself, turning over the idea of otherness as she went up to her bedroom. She rather liked the idea of being 'other'.

Early start tomorrow. The 'closed' sign would be hanging on the door; another day of stocktaking, her least favourite part of owning Persephone's. Her nubby old bedroom carpet was threadbare at the threshold. It needed replacing but when would she ever find the time? There was always something else more urgent: processing book deliveries and returns, refreshing tired old displays, working through customer orders and reservations. She went into the bathroom. Strange how the air in here felt colder than the rest of the house. She'd set the timer for the central heating and the bathroom radiator was blasting heat out like all hell's fires – it was almost too hot to touch – but still there was that damp chill in the room.

65

A sickening, degrading cold?

She squeezed a hefty blob of bright blue toothpaste onto her brush and looked at herself in the mirror. She was still handsome, although the lines on her face were getting a little deeper each year. They gave her an air of authority, she thought; she looked august, professorial even. She was certainly in the right city for that. She raised the toothbrush to her mouth – paused – looked mildly surprised, then stared hard into the mirror, leaning in a little, watching two small handprints form on the misty surface of the glass, like a child's fingers pressing into clay or the icing of a cake.

And then the mirror shatters.

Freya flinches and turns away instinctively to protect her face, snapping her eyes shut. She expects splintered shards, flying glass. But there is nothing. After a moment, she turns back towards the glass, opening one eye gingerly. The entire mirror is cracked like ice on a frozen pond. Now she hears a sound from the hallway, a distant rumbling, a frenzied rattling. She puts her toothbrush down carefully beside the sink and steps onto the landing. The sound is coming from her bedroom. She presses her palm against the door and slowly pushes it open.

The furniture is shaking as if moved by invisible hands. Lamps spin and fall. The frame of the bed vibrates as if supercharged with electricity. A small pile of books shuffles towards the edge of the bedside table, tips over, and collapses onto the carpet. A chair with clothes thrown carelessly across its back – a pair of lime green socks, dungarees, a colour-washed tee, a straw hat – tips over and the clothes are strewn in a jumble across the floor. Freya watches a vase of daffodils dance across the dresser. The dresser's drawers rattle and cackle on their sliders, lunging forwards like angry dogs. Before Freya can reach it, the vase tips over, spilling its contents: flowers fall, water runs across the polished wood and darkens the carpet. The bedroom door slams shut with an emphatic crack.

Then, just like that, everything stops.

Freya stands the vase back up and looks around the room. She perches on the edge of the bed, and murmurs to herself, 'Oh, my word.'

v

Preet had said hardly anything at the book group, and she knew the others had noticed. She picked up a picture from her desk; it was her mother holding a baby in her arms, both of them smiling, the small child grinning ecstatically at the camera, contented, alive. That baby was not Preet. It was her sister Mahi. When Preet was seven years old, Mahi had died suddenly. Cot death. The story of *Beloved* had affected Preet more than she cared to admit – the death of a child was a slice of her own reality, hard to confront.

She'd loved the brief time she'd had with Mahi, making funny faces, playing peekaboo; watching her giggle and wiggle her tiny toes and fingers. Then one morning she was gone and the silence in the house became a roar of agony. She didn't fully understand what had happened; her parents said Mahi had simply gone away, to be reborn. She watched her mother sitting in her big green armchair, staring into space; her father busying himself with little jobs around the house. For a while, it was almost as if Preet had vanished too. It was like mum and dad couldn't see her anymore. Weeks and months went by, and gradually they came back to her. Later, another baby was born, a boy this time. But every now and again, over the years, Preet would stop and wonder what Mahi would have been like if she had lived. What her favourite game would have been? Her favourite colour? Her favourite ice cream? The places she'd choose to run and play; the songs she'd sing?

Preet went straight up to her room as soon as she got back to halls. She lay on the bed, listening to Baby Queen and Hayley Kiyoko on her headphones. She contemplated starting *Not After Midnight*, the next book on the reading list; perhaps it would be a way of putting *Beloved* behind her. But she found herself reaching for *Beloved* instead of the du Maurier – she wasn't really a fan of short stories. She began reading *Beloved* from the beginning, all over again.

That night she dreams of Mahi. She is singing in the blackness outside Preet's window, calling out her name. The sound is beautiful, a siren call. Preet has no choice; she must go to her, follow her song in spite of the biting cold. She runs into dense autumnal woods where fallen leaves, dead on the earth, snap and crunch under her feet; Mahi's voice seems further away, a whisper on the wind.

Preet redoubles her efforts, running faster and faster to keep pace with the sound of the song, but the words are indistinct and she realises her feet are bare and the ground is hard and deathly cold. She can just make out a figure in the distance and then it is gone. She drops to her knees, chest tight. She is by a lake now; water stagnant; everything dead. And there is the figure at the water's edge.

Preet reaches out and strokes the girl's long silken hair.

She is young, probably in her teens. She is wearing a plain white cotton nightdress. She turns and she has the face of a million other girls. She reaches into her mouth and pulls out a tooth, turning it over in her hand; studying it in awe.

'Does it hurt?' Preet says.

'Yes.'

'Then why don't you cry?'

chapter four

"Incredibly, he felt no pain, his mind too numbed by terror and shock for the message to reach his brain."

THE RATS | JAMES HERBERT

*Its corpse-skin fascinates
and repels him.*

i

A corner table looking out over Prospect Row. A window on the world. The smell of warm beer and roasting beef; the Sunday lunchtime chatter of friends, old and new. Hard to believe The Free Press was founded as one big joke, taking its name from the temperance movement's anti-drinking newspaper – first edition: 1834. The paper lasted one issue, the pub nearly two centuries. Still going strong. Its fiercely loyal clientele saw to that, loyalists that included Freya Bancroft and Sebastian Sizemore.

'So, Mister Big Shot Author, why have you been hiding

away?' Freya said. 'People have been asking after you. You missed *Beloved*, and *I Am Legend*. I thought you loved Richard Matheson.'

'My dear woman, I knew the man! *Duel* was his best work. Much better than the film. Though *Legend* is a jolly good romp.'

'Nancy wasn't keen. She's not a lover of zombies.'

'But it's hardly a zombie story is it?'

'I suppose not. The Will Smith film made it seem that way.'

Sebastian leaned across his pint of Guinness, fixing her with a professorial stare: 'The film is hardly the book. Filmmakers take the most awful liberties with a text.'

'You haven't answered my question, darling. What have you been doing to keep you away from The Shirley Jackson Club? Beavering away on the new novel, I'm guessing?'

'It's going splendidly, better than I could have hoped. It's like it used to be all those years ago. The words are just flowing out. I'm back!'

'I'm assuming that first edition of *We Have Always Lived in the Castle* helped!' Freya said.

'More than you could possibly imagine. But the mirror was the thing.' He looked a little distant for a moment as if he held an age-old secret and it amused him to keep it.

'Why the mirror?' Freya asked but she had the strangest feeling she wasn't going to like the answer.

'I've been getting help from the great mistress of horror herself!' Sebastian's secret was out. 'I ask her how I should go on with each chapter and she tells me.'

'Just to be clear,' Freya said, 'exactly who are we talking about?'

'Shirley Jackson, of course. She speaks to me. She guides me.'

'You're channelling her?' Freya Bancroft had seen it all before: seances, table rapping, speaking in tongues. She didn't doubt the truth of Sebastian's words. Nor did she doubt the benevolent nature of unseen forces if summoned in the correct way. But she also understood the importance of protection when dealing with those forces. 'You took the necessary precautions, didn't you?' She took an emphatic swig of her gin and tonic and smacked it down on the table, looking a little sternly at her friend.

Sebastian waved a dismissive hand.

'Of course, dear girl.'

'You did some smudging, used a talisman, that sort of thing?'

'Yes, yes, yes,' Sebastian said with another more impatient wave. 'You're looking at the wrong part of the picture. The important thing is that I've been racing along, almost finished the book. The real genius was the clown motif. I liked the Pennywise figure in the Stephen King novel, so I incorporated a killer clown into my own. Clowns are terrifying, don't you think?' He reached into his satchel and pulled out a thick manila envelope. 'This is the current draft. I'm still working on the last three chapters. I'd like you to read it before anyone else.'

'I'd be honoured.' Freya regarded the packet reverently before placing it carefully beside her.

'Enough about me,' said Sebastian. 'Tell me about you and the charming, but enigmatic, Ms Judy Miller.'

'Judy's been great. She's a regular at the Shirley Jackson Club, which is more than I can say for some people.' Freya smiled.

'That's not what I'm asking, dear girl, and you know it.'

'We're getting along very well. Two old ducks among the dreaming spires, so to speak. We've been for tea and Chelsea buns at Fitzbillies a few times and we've taken a couple of walks along the Cam.'

'And is this a purely platonic bond?'

'At the moment,' Freya said, taking a less emphatic sip of her drink.

'I hope it all works out wonderfully for you both, whatever it turns out to be. Now I have to dash.' He raised his pint of Guinness in a salutary gesture, and drained the remaining liquid. 'I feel revitalised and refreshed and I can feel the old creative juices flowing. I'll be finishing those last few chapters any day now.'

ii

The nights had drawn in rapidly, relentlessly it seemed to Judy, as autumn faded. Judy had never liked the winter; the dark always felt interminable to her and even more unforgiving since Greta died. She dreaded the evenings; sunset before 4pm, sitting alone in her house. The Shirley Jackson Club was something to look forward to; a bright point in the dying of the light. Her breath condensed on the window at Bridges café as she watched car headlights moving down the street, pitched against the encroaching dark. Buses trundled by, their interiors harsh with fluorescent light, following their designated routes doggedly around the city. They were like engines on a children's train set, Judy thought.

A huge black rat bares its teeth, curls its razor-sharp claws, ready to seize its next victim.

Its feeding ground – London – is pictured as a forlorn and filthy silhouette in the distance.

When Judy first saw the cover of *The Rats* she knew she would hate the book. It was too violent, too gruesome. A one-year-old baby is eaten alive in the opening chapters, for goodness sake! What a thing to put in a story! *The Rats* put her in mind of another book they'd read at the group, *The Woods Are Dark*; dreadful pulp, she thought; a bunch of cannibals living in the forests of the American Midwest. By Richard Lurman? Richard Longman? *The Rats* reminded her too much of that one. Over the top. Unnecessary. Although she had to admit, it would have made a sensational blockbuster movie. Had they made a film of it? She'd look it up when she got home or ask lovely Tom. He was bound to know. So here Judy was, in her favourite spot in Bridges at her usual time, just half an hour before the start of the Shirley Jackson Club.

'Oh, *The Rats*!' the waitress said. 'Is it any good?'

'Don't read it if you're just about to eat,' Judy laughed.

The waitress took her order and Judy was struck suddenly by how much this little routine of the café and the book club had become part of her life this past month or so. She'd already got to know the waitress – Lola from Leeds – now in her second year of study, living with her boyfriend in a student house share just off Mill Road. She mostly worked at the café outside of term time but she had taken Judy under her wing, putting a little reserved sign on Judy's spot by the window, asking about her week and what book they were doing at the group. Judy was becoming increasingly *au fait* with the world of horror fiction. She never thought she'd say it but some of the books were really rather good, and certainly more thought-provoking than most people gave them credit for. She'd enjoyed *Beloved, Frankenstein* and *The Haunting of Hill House*. They had substance, a psychological aspect, a certain elegance to the way they evoked foreboding. But she didn't hold out much hope for Mr James Herbert's bloodthirsty potboiler, *The Rats*. It struck her as beyond the pale.

iii

Shirley Jackson Club Meeting:
***The Rats* – James Herbert.**
Cardboard boxes are stacked precariously at one end of the room. The books inside must wait for their time in the light – to be fanned out on display tables or, if they are 'the chosen ones' to be spotlit on individual bookstands. Foolscap folders and files form an uneven mountain range beside these boxes and perched on top, strange as it seems, are a couple of Ping-Pong bats. Two small convector heaters, plugged into opposite walls, buzz furiously as they fight the good fight against the chill from the exposed brickwork. Brownish stains on the ceiling tell eloquent tales of creeping damp or a leaky pipe.

Not long after they met, Freya told Judy owning a bookshop was the least certain route to making one's fortune; she was in it for passion, not money. To be surrounded by so many authors and all their pooled wisdom was a reassuring way to live. And ditto that satisfying 'ding, ding, ding,' of the bell over the door, announcing the arrival of a new customer, someone who shared those same passions, someone who might become a friend. Then, of course, there were the crazy kids who dreamed of working in an occult bookshop, thought it all very *Harry Potter*, but had never actually read a book of their own volition. ('I follow someone on TikTok who does reviews, she's really good.') And why were these youngsters always such heavy drinkers?

Now glasses have been passed around and filled, the last of the candles lit. Freya encourages the chatterers – Nancy, Preet, Leon – to take their seats.

Judy was jolted out of her reverie by Nancy's elbow. The girl was fumbling absentmindedly in her bag for *The Rats*. 'Jeepers, sorry about that! I really must get my life sorted out!'

She's a strange girl, thought Judy, always forgetting her copy of whatever they were reading, bumblingly energetic, supremely disorganised. Judy couldn't imagine how she was going to make it through three years at Cambridge University. But then again, she'd met plenty of supremely intelligent and gifted people who were supremely disorganised, and they usually muddled through in the end. Often they were unorganised precisely because there was so much going on inside their heads. 'Don't worry,' Judy said, 'you can share mine. Perhaps you could choose a spot at home where you always keep your book for book club. Then you'd never mislay it.'

'It's finding a space among all my junk,' Nancy said, snapping her bag shut and looking up at Judy.

She has the most lustrous eyes, like dark Tahitian pearls, Judy thought. Absolutely beautiful.

'What did you think of the book?' Nancy asked.

Judy doesn't have time to answer; Freya is calling the group together and beginning her customary plot summary: 'Published in 1974, *The Rats* was an instant success and spawned three sequels: *Lair* in 1979, *Domain* in 1984, and also a graphic novel in the 1990s, although I can't remember the exact year. The plot is quite straightforward: people in London are being attacked by abnormally large rats. The rat-bites are infectious, killing the victims within twenty-four hours. The rats grow rapidly in number and begin to swarm. The government implements emergency procedures to tackle the crisis amid a public outcry.'

'It was groundbreaking when it came out,' Tom said. 'Very different from the usual horror fiction of the early seventies, at least for British horror. It was much more violent and graphic. Some said Herbert threw away the rule book when he wrote it.'

'I should say so,' Judy said. 'I thought it was far too graphic.'

'Me too,' said Nancy. 'Rats and zombies don't do it for me, I'm afraid. I like a good singular monster, or ghost. One of a kind.'

'Like *Frankenstein*?' Tom said.

'Now there's a book!' Nancy said, grinning.

'I thought *The Rats* was very cinematic,' Judy said. 'Was it ever made into a film, Tom?'

'*Deadly Eyes* in 1982. Canadian, set in Toronto, I think. Not a huge box office hit. James Herbert wasn't very pleased with it. I think he described it as a terrible load of rubbish. Apparently the characters are poorly drawn and the dialogue's appalling. I haven't got hold of a copy yet, but I intend to.' He looked at his three fellow students with a gleeful smile.

'Getting back to the book,' Freya said, a little teacherishly. 'Tom's right, *The Rats* is considered a British horror classic. Neil Gaiman said he thought it changed the face of horror publishing in the UK. And Ramsey Campbell, another great British horror writer, felt it broke away from the tired old clichés of the 1970s.'

'It's a take on the idea of Original Sin, isn't it?' Nancy said.

'I'm not sure how religious Herbert was himself,' said Tom.

'The social commentary is pretty clear,' Preet said. 'The rats are overrunning London and the authorities are pretty ineffectual in dealing with them.'

'The rats attack the vulnerable,' Leon said. 'People living on the edge of society or who have dropped off the radar and been left to rot. The rats attack the homeless, at first.'

'Herbert was conscious of social divisions,' Freya said. 'He came from a working class background and grew up in London after the Second World War. A lot of the city was bombed out and was left that way for years.'

She was interrupted by the sound of footsteps. Sebastian threw out his arms like a star greeting fans at the stage door.

'The prodigal son returns,' Freya laughed. 'I was beginning to think you weren't coming.' She poured a huge glass of red wine and handed it to him.

'I wouldn't miss a James Herbert for the world,' he said. 'Lived in Woodford Green when I knew him. Charming daughters.'

'So where have you been hiding?' Preet asked.

'I've been grafting away on my new novel. And, I'm very happy to say, it's finished.' He raised his glass in a toast to himself then bowed theatrically at the little medley of congratulations.

'And are you going to tell us what it's about?' Preet said.

'It has a little bit of everything,' Sebastian said. 'A haunted house, a ghostly child, a killer clown. Freya has read it, apart from the final chapters. But she's under strict instructions to keep schtum.' Freya offered them all a sweet, tightlipped smile.

iv

Sebastian quickened his pace. The air was clean and crisp. He passed a young couple, arm in arm, huddled against the cold on King's Parade. Sebastian had enjoyed the book club, always enjoyed Freya's company, and he liked the walk home; it made for good thinking time.

'Come on, let's have a look at it, then.'

Sebastian was ten years old. It was the middle of July, thick green leaves dancing in the bright light. His cousin Roddy was staying for a couple of weeks (Roddy's parents had gone to Spain, leaving him behind; a last, desperate bid to patch up their rocky marriage). Roddy was older and tougher than Sebastian. A difficult-to-describe bleakness clung about him: square head, thick neck, broad shoulders. He had inclinations towards a career in the army; a good influence for Seb, his parents thought. Seb was too ethereal, too ungrounded, always with his nose in a book. Seb needed to toughen up or the world would eat him alive. His parents didn't know it but Roddy was a disastrous choice for playmate. Roddy was a vicious inveterate bully. When Sebastian's parents weren't looking, he tormented and humiliated Seb, every chance he got.

'Go and play. Take a ball with you and have a kick about,' Sebastian's father said from behind *The Telegraph*.

As they strolled onto the playing fields behind the house, Roddy stripped a branch from a young tree, pushed Sebastian to the ground, and whipped his buttocks with it...

There was an uncanny silence in the city tonight. A hurricane's eye. The air nipped at Sebastian's face and hands.

'Let's smack your arse, you useless little bum boy!' Roddy turned Sebastian onto his back and sat on him, slapping his face now. Then he bounced the heavy football on Sebastian's forehead. 'You can't even kick a ball properly, you bloody little sissy! Bet you've got a pussy instead of a dick.'

'I have got a dick!'

'Shut up!' Another smack to the face. 'Girlies should use nice words.' This, followed by a jab in the ribs with pointed fingers. 'Girly-boys like you don't have willies.'

'I do too!' Sebastian's face was hot and wet with tears.

'Prove it!'

Sebastian fumbled with his fly, but Roddy was already pulling down his shorts, tugging down his underpants.

'Not much there.' Roddy stared gleefully at him, grabbing his penis, squeezing and twisting. Sebastian let out a stuck-pig squeal. 'Aw, are we gonna cry now?' Roddy punched him in the stomach. Sebastian threw up. 'Yuk! You're so disgusting Sissy-bastian. I'm going back. I don't play football with sissy boys.'

Sebastian wondered why the incident with Roddy – a lifetime ago – was playing on his mind now. In the end, Roddy didn't join the military. He took over his father's construction business, got married, had the obligatory two-point-four children and drank himself to death.

Bravo! But those times with Roddy had stayed with him. Roddy's accusations had no grain of truth in them; Sebastian never had the remotest inclination in that direction apart from the odd wanking competition at summer camp with a very handsome older boy called, magnificently, Hubie Lord. But that could hardly be described as a gay experience. In those days, any boy who didn't fit into the 'fighting, fucking, and football' paradigm was automatically labelled a bender.

Sebastian walked and thought. He was going over the final chapter of his new book: the climactic encounter with the killer clown. Stephen King's *It* had wrong-footed him, bringing back these uncomfortable memories from childhood. He hadn't been able to get *It* out of his mind ever since reading the book for the Shirley Jackson Club. The stink of death, something waiting, ready to feed on the innocent; that's what had brought back these awful memories of Roddy. There was a homophobic attack, a killing, right at the beginning of King's novel: the murder of a young gay man, Adrian Mellon, under a bridge. And then there were the other kids, the misfits, the losers, victims of the bullies, just like himself at that age: stuttering Bill Denbrough, Beverly Marsh, Richie Tozier. The evil was always lurking, waiting to get to them. It bided its time. It chose its moment.

Show me your cock, queer, and I'll cut it off for you!

It had left him in a dark place when he should have been feeling on top of the world. He'd just finished his great comeback, his magnum opus; that was cause for celebration not dismay. The great S.J. Sizemore was back better than ever! He'd show them, the bloody critics, looking down their noses at his life's work: Brian

Alderson, John Carey, Aileen Pippett, and the rest. The whole miserable bloody lot of them.

Sebastian needed a drink to warm him against the cold of this night and his memories. He dug deep into his cavernous coat pocket. He pulled out *The Rats* along with some old till receipts from Berry Bros. & Rudd. How long had they been in there? He remembered what a seismic jolt there had been when *The Rats* was first published back in November 1974. Killing a baby in the opening chapters! That was a gamble but also pure genius. Herbert changed the whole genre with this one and never looked back. James Herbert – you cheeky little tinker. God bless you, sir!

Sebastian had chosen his favourite spot at The Eagle, next to the large marble fireplace: a quick glass of Lanson then he'd head on home. He always delighted in the mix of punters. Tonight: a group of young women, probably students, enjoying a few glasses of bubbly before going on somewhere else to eat; two elderly professors talking animatedly about Dostoyevsky, Turgenev and Tolstoy; a trio of American tourists in baseball caps and sweatshirts flicking through their city guides, while downing pints of Eagle's DNA. It was hard to believe that here, on the 28th of February 1953, Watson and Crick announced to startled lunchtime drinkers that they had discovered 'the secret of life' or, more prosaically, the structure of deoxyribonucleic acid. Freya would be quick to remind him that it was Rosalind Franklin, chemist and crystallographer, whose unpublished data paved the way for Watson and Crick's discovery. They wouldn't have stood a chance without her brilliant photographs, revealing the structure for anyone to see. Freya would also note that Franklin was often left out of the narrative because she was a woman. 'It took a woman's eye,' she'd say with a few stabs of the finger into his lapel. Sebastian smiled to himself. Fiery, opinionated, and he loved her for it.

Bene't Street was deserted as Sebastian left The Eagle. The Stephen King book was back on his mind again. What was the name of the gay bar in the story? Was it The Eagle? The Buzzard? The Hawk? The Vulture? No, no. The Falcon! There wasn't a gay bar in Cambridge, was there? He'd never heard of one. He'd seen a flier for a gay group once on the railings around All Saints Garden. It was one of the thousands of fliers advertising everything from piano concertos to disco yoga: 'Shake your Chakras!' That was the thing about Cambridge. Everything was here. Everyone was here.

Evil is also here. Age-old evil. Hiding, watching, waiting. Waiting for you, Sebastian Sizemore. You no-good, book-loving little ponce.

The waters of the Cam are silvery under the moonlight, the river a mass of shifting glass. Somewhere an owl hoots. On Jesus Green, Sebastian passes the lido on his way to Victoria Bridge. The breeze whistles through the trees. The air sharpens a fraction more as he walks along the narrow towpath. There isn't another soul around. He approaches the bridge, and here we go: a desperate cry, repeated, 'Help! Help! They're killing him! Help!'

Sebastian hurries.

Then, the sound of other voices: 'Bum's rush! Bum's rush! Over the side!'

A young man is struggling against two youths on the bridge. They are punching him. Now they are hauling him over the side of the bridge. Now he is falling into the ice-cold water.

'Stop!' Sebastian yells and the youths turn to look at him; then they are gone, vanished into the night.

The boy splutters as he swims uncertainly towards the river bank. Before Sebastian can get to him, something very large hauls the boy out of the water. Sissy-boy Seb moves as quickly as he can but, when he gets there, both the young man and the something very large are gone. The passage from the King book: the attack under the bridge, the murder of Ade Mellon.

Bum's rush! Bum's rush!

Maybe this is a re-enactment. Maybe it's a student prank like the time they suspended an Austin 7 from the Bridge of Sighs in '63, or propped up a Fiat on stilts in the middle of the river in the mid-80s, or put Santa hats on the pinnacles of King's College chapel. Just a prank; a bunch of drunken literature majors larking about.

Something shifts now in the shadow underneath the bridge. Something crouching, now rising. Something huge.

A clown.

Pennywise from the King novel, except it isn't. It's like a clown but full of imperfections; a half-remembered idea of a clown; an almost-clown; a skewed image; something seen through a broken window streaked with dirt. Its shoes are too small; its clothes too neatly patterned and arranged, and it has claw-fingers with grey scales and thick, sharp nails like a rat's.

The almost-clown steps out from under the godforsaken bridge. Sebastian's heart is in his throat. He can't catch his breath. How can this be happening? A nightmare from the pages of a book.

It can't be Pennywise. Am I suffering from a lesion on the brain? A haemorrhage? A seizure?

'It isn't him, it isn't him!' He shuts his eyes and opens them again and the clown thing is still coming towards him, as if drawn badly by a child, a shoddy estimation, a freakish almost-but-not-quite clown. It can't be but it is, here in the chill night by the bridge over the Cam.

They float. Down here we all float.

Its corpse-skin – Mehron white – fascinates and repulses him. He is the deep sea diver staring rigidly into the jaws of a great white.

Sebastian Sizemore, master of horror, is a frightened child again, a little boy having his pants pulled down by his bullying cousin, his cock squeezed and twisted. The unholy apparition pulls him close and its thick nails tear his old-man's flesh – so easily torn – thin as tomato skin. His face, his neck, his arms are running red. The almost-clown takes him now. Sebastian opens his mouth in a scream that never comes. His terrified stare fixes on something: a solitary red balloon caught under the arch of the bridge, edging its way slowly towards him like a mouse sniffing out a piece of cheese. And, as it rolls and twists against the brickwork, he can just make out writing on its side: *I HEART DERRY*. Now a breath of wind catches the balloon and takes it swiftly up into the night sky, over the crumpled form of Sebastian Sizemore, over the still-savage green of the common, over the rooftops of the colleges and dormitories of Cambridge University, and into the streets of the city. Poor lost and lonely balloon, waiting for so long, searching for so long. Searching now for another victim.

chapter five

"The blood flowed across the page and began to drip onto the floor."
IT | STEPHEN KING

*Venice was like a beautiful mask
with a ruined face underneath.*

i

She'd spoken to the nurse about the patient's condition and was on her way out when she ran into the two women. One had a mane of thick, grey hair and an assortment of necklaces over a paisley maxi-dress. The other was petite, ash-blonde, dressed more conservatively.

'Are you relatives?' Detective Inspector Lena Sorensen asked.

'We're just friends of Sebastian's,' the grey-haired woman said, 'from his book group. I'm Freya Bancroft and this is Judy Miller. Is he going to be all right?'

'I'm afraid he hasn't regained consciousness yet. It was

a very serious attack.'

'Do you have any idea who did it?'

'The details are very sketchy. All we know is that a man walking his dog heard shouting and found Mr Sizemore lying unconscious under Victoria Bridge. The victim's neck and chest had been slashed but luckily the man who found him was a nurse – he works here at the hospital – and was able to minister critical first aid at the scene.'

'That was very fortunate,' the ash-blonde said.

'Indeed. Let's hope Mr Sizemore regains consciousness and is able to identify his attacker.' With an abrupt goodbye, DI Sorensen headed down the corridor.

Judy followed Freya into the small hospital room. The lights were turned down and the odour of disinfectant suggested the floor had been freshly mopped. Sebastian, always so full of life, looked small and broken under the white bedsheets. A tube ran from his arm to an intravenous drip and wires connected him to a monitor which beeped intermittently. The left side of his face was bandaged, as were his neck and chest. He put Judy in mind of an animal rescued from the roadside where it had been left to die.

'Oh dear,' Freya said and her eyes filled with tears. Judy took hold of her hand and they sat down beside the bed. 'Whoever could do this to another human being?'

'I don't know,' was all Judy could say.

'He was so excited about his book,' Freya said. 'His *great big knock 'em dead comeback*, he called it.'

'Did you read the manuscript he gave you?'

'Yes, I read it as soon as I got home. I couldn't wait to see what he'd been up to.'

'And?'

Freya's smile seemed a little forced. 'It didn't seem like something he'd write. Not really his style. A lot of elements borrowed from other books, some we'd read at the group: a haunted house, a killer clown, a mad scientist stitching body parts.'

'It sounds a bit disjointed.'

Freya stared down at Sebastian: 'Poor old stick. Maybe a good editor could have blue-pencilled it into something workable. Sebastian has quite a cult following for his early work. A clever publisher could have pulled out all the stops to make the new S.J. Sizemore a modern classic. Let's hope Sebastian comes back to us. I'd miss his funny ways. It mustn't end like this.'

'I'm sure we'll all be sitting together in a few months time, drinking wine and discussing *Dracula* or *Dr Jekyll and Mr Hyde*. Or some other gruesome tale you've dug up for us.' Judy tried to sound as reassuring as she could.

'I need to think about the next books for the club,' Freya said, trying to distract herself. 'We're coming to the end of the current list with the du Maurier.'

'I had no idea Daphne du Maurier wrote horror.'

'She's often overlooked. *Just a romantic novelist*, people say but she wrote some terrific horror and science fiction stories. *Don't Look Now* is probably the most famous.'

They were both silent for a while, then Freya said, 'Are you hungry? We really should get something to eat but not here at the hospital. I can't face it, thinking of poor Sebastian lying in that bed.'

The Ketton stone of King's College glowed amber under the streetlights, the tall arches flanking the foregate flushed with shades of fiery orange. Judy contemplated King's through the wide glass frontage of the Chop House; she could well have been looking at the *Castle of Otranto*. That was the one horror novel she'd read at Middlesex Poly. It was part of her foundation course and the only horror novel she'd ever read before joining the Shirley Jackson Club. She couldn't remember very much about it apart from the sentiment that it was the original gothic novel, setting the tone for the rest to come. Lots of damsels in distress and ghostly apparitions. As they looked at the menu distractedly, Freya ordered them two large glasses of wine 'for medicinal purposes'.

They were both quiet, thinking about Sebastian.

Freya broke the silence. 'I usually find this time of year in Cambridge magical,' she said. 'The clear dark skies, the students broken up for the holidays, the streets hushed and chilly and empty. It's almost like a different city.'

'A little breathing space,' Judy added, 'the lull before the festive storm. What do witches do for Christmas?'

'We definitely don't sing songs to the baby Jesus and we don't call it Christmas. We celebrate Yule on the 21st of December, the winter solstice. I usually burn a candle at sunset and then one at sunrise.'

'Excuse my ignorance, but why?'

'To celebrate the death of the sun god and then his rebirth. It heralds the beginning of the fertile season. It's a tradition dating back to the Stone Age.'

'The more I get to know you, the more whole worlds open up to me!'

'You have an English degree. You're far from being an ignoramus.'

'My degree's not from Cambridge, just plain old Middlesex Poly, as it was in those days.'

'Well neither is mine, and so bloody what?' Freya said. 'You worked hard for it, didn't you? A degree's a degree at the end of the day. I'm sure you had more fun than the poor hamsters on the Cambridge University wheel. I can picture you now: radical leftwing meetings, lesbian discos, student marches and demos. I bet you had a whale of a time.'

Judy's smile was Delphic. 'I might have dabbled a bit. It was in the air. My girlfriend at college was a member of the SWP.'

Freya sighed contentedly, 'The SWP! Those were the days. These Cambridge kids wouldn't know a socialist worker if he jumped up and bit them on the arse.' It felt good to be talking to Judy. Judy Miller with her neatly pressed blouse and ash-blonde hair had no idea just how beguiling she was, and that made her all the more so.

The thought struck Freya from nowhere: Sebastian had shared his manuscript with her first, something intimate for any author to do and now he might never see it published. She felt so terribly sad. 'Getting back to the subject of Christmas,' she said, 'what are your plans for the tinsel tsunami?'

Judy twisted the stem of her wine glass thoughtfully. 'When Greta was alive, we often held a small party just before Christmas, nothing formal, professors and university staff, somewhere around the 21st of December, the time you'd be lighting your candles. Needless to say, we avoided inviting George and Martha! They'd usually gone back to the States by then.' She laughed, a forced, half-laugh. 'Last year was my first Christmas without Greta. I was invited out by a lot of well-meaning people but I just wanted to be alone. I made a promise to myself to grit my teeth and get through it, read a lot, cry a lot, watch a lot of old movies and hope it was over as quickly as possible.'

Freya listened in silence, her expression unaltered. There was a weary composure in Judy's face, a dignified pain, and Freya wanted to ease that pain, if she could.

'It must have been unbearable,' she said. 'Everybody makes such a bloody song and dance about Christmas, specially people who aren't remotely religious.'

'Don't they just? And if you're on your own you're made to feel a pitiable failure.'

'If being a failure means avoiding ghastly family get-togethers, I'm all for failing!' Freya said. 'What d'you think's the most un-Christmas meal you can have?'

'Beans on toast?' Judy offered. 'Chicken curry? Crispy duck? Anything but turkey!'

'And what's the most un-Christmas film?'

'*Frankenstein*?'

'Perfect,' said Freya. 'What say we get together on Christmas Day for chicken curry and *Frankenstein*? We can celebrate being total festive failures together.'

Judy thought about it. Freya seemed to dance hand in hand with mischief, always ready to cock a snook at the rest of the world and its conventions. And she was right, why should Judy be home alone, wishing the days away? Boris Karloff and a Balti with a warm and witty witch seemed like a wonderful alternative. Judy felt a little lighter suddenly. She raised her glass to Freya. 'Let's do it.'

'How come you're a girl?' the boy said, looking at Preet dubiously as if she'd landed from Venus slap bang on the banks of the Cam.

'Girls can be coxes, too,' she told him. She guessed he must be about ten years old and she'd seen him hanging around the yard before. She'd tried to talk to him then, but each time he'd turned on his heels and marched away. This afternoon was last practice for St Benedict's College Boat Club before the holidays. She'd arrived just after the boy, cutting off his escape route so he was forced to stand his ground.

'But all the rowers are boys,' he said, almost accusingly. 'Bet they don't take any notice of you.'

'You'd be surprised. I have a pretty big voice,' she said smiling. 'They have to take notice: I'm responsible for steering the boat and for the safety of the crew. There are lots of women who are coxes. It's often better to have a woman cox than a man.'

'Why?' He wrinkled his nose.

'Often women weigh less than men, which means there's less weight for the crew to carry.' The boy looked over the water, the surface rippling in the cold breeze. 'Do you like being by the river?' she asked. He nodded. 'Would you like to be a cox one day?'

'No, it's a girl's job.'

'So you want to be a rower, then?'

The boy nodded again.

'Why don't I have a word with the team captain? See if we can't get you some jobs to do? Would you like that?'

The boy hesitated, shy suddenly, glancing down at the ground. 'I'd have to ask my mum.'

'No problem,' Preet said with a wink. 'I'm sure I can get our team captain to take notice of me and we can definitely find plenty of things for you to do.'

'Like what?'

'Tidying up, making cups of tea, washing the team's kit.' The boy looked horrified. Preet laughed. 'Just kidding. We can certainly use someone for checking equipment and making sure everything gets put back in the right place.'

'Okay.'

'What's your name?'

'Tom.'

'I'm Preet. I have a friend called Tom. He's very nice.' The boy looked up at her, brightening. She nudged his cheek with her hand. 'And now I guess I've got two.'

iv

The noise from the jet engines was suddenly less. Tom took a deep breath and tried to relax. This was the part he hated most: when the plane levels off after climbing 30,000 ft into the sky. At this moment he always felt the cabin was about to buck and tip and plummet back to earth, tumbling apart in a ragged shower of flame and twisted metal. He was digging his fingers deep into the fabric of the arm rests. The flight from Heathrow to Dublin would take one-and-a-quarter hours. Then it was a four hour coach ride to Killarrey. He invariably felt like a rusty old robot – oil-starved, stiff and creaking – when he clambered off the bus at the other end. He'd left St Benedict's College in the dark and he would arrive at his parents' house in the dark as well. The night before, he'd been on a mammoth end-of-term pub crawl with Preet,

Nancy and Leon. They came back very late, very loud and very happy, and then it was all laid to waste when they received Freya's message at the porter's lodge: *Sebastian was attacked last night on his way home from the group. He's in a coma in Addenbrooke's Hospital.*

Tom barely recognised his own voice. Everything that came out of his mouth sounded like a banality. What do you say in the face of something like that? They sat in the kitchen, drinking strong coffee; none of them really knowing what to say. Tom thought about being young, how far removed it seemed from even the idea of death. But, in truth, anyone's life could be snuffed out just like that. It makes no difference if you're 18 or 80, all you really have is this moment, this day. They were all leaving halls in the morning: Preet back to Manchester, Leon to London, Tom to Ireland. Only Nancy, helping out at her family's Japanese restaurant on Mill Road, would be able to visit Sebastian. Tom slept in Leon's bed; a last night together before the horrible ache of separation. The radio startled them awake at 6am: Joel Mitchell's *Early Breakfast* was far too early.

The patchwork of fields looked very small from the aircraft window. High above the Home Counties, Tom felt his shoulders relax at last. He was safe (for now at least) and on his way home. His mother had planned a huge family party for his return. Everyone was encouraged to come and see the great Cambridge scholar and listen to his adventures. In truth, he spent all of his time going to lectures, wading through piles of books, doing supervision work. Now and again, he was able to watch old horror movies with Leon, Preet and Nancy, or eat at formals. or go to the university LGBT group (but that was top secret where his family were concerned). He was never comfortable being the centre of attention. Neither of his older brothers went to university. Both Sean and Niall were already married and subsumed into his father's decorating and maintenance business. Now that was a fate worse than death.

But Thomas Aiden Donnelly, son of self-made man and salt-of-the-earth Brendan Donnelly, was an undergraduate at one of the most prestigious universities in the world. (How had he managed that? He still had to pinch himself sometimes.) He was also a gay man, though not a soul at home knew. His family were traditional, churchgoing folk; mass every Sunday; midnight mass on Christmas Eve; a manger on the mantelpiece; statues of the Blessed Virgin in every corner of the house; a tinsel-choked fir tree towering over the living room. The reputation of Cambridge students for working hard served him well. He told everyone he was concentrating on his studies; no time for a girlfriend. He intended to tell them the truth eventually, when the time was right, when he had a publishing job in London and a place to live, maybe a place he and Leon had chosen together. When he was able to stand on his own two feet, an independent man, he'd tell them then.

He got an uneasy feeling, like falling over, when he thought about it. His father, a bad-tempered bear of a man with ruddy cheeks and a gin-flower nose, was infamous for brawling in the local pubs. He had flown into a rage at Tom's brother, Sean, blackening an eye and almost breaking a cheekbone, and all because Sean had got a girl pregnant out of wedlock. Tom had always been afraid of his father; of his growl of a voice; the thick black hairs on the backs of his fists; his thick lips and broken nose; his oh-so-volatile temper. A man as hard as iron.

Tom wanted his Cambridge degree, his ticket to a new life, so desperately. And he didn't want any family strife getting in the way.

He dreaded the plane's descent and final approach through the clouds; hoary cotton wool outside the window and half-expecting the wool to part and another jetliner to appear, screaming towards them. For God's sake, he thought, we're not even halfway there yet and you're already imagining midair collisions. He ordered a double whisky and ginger, then another. His nerves started to settle down nicely.

The Cambridge press were saying the attack on Sebastian was unprovoked. Sebastian's wallet was still on him with the cash and credit cards all accounted for. How could anyone strike Sebastian down for no reason? Tom was in awe of Sebastian. Whenever the elderly author came to the group, Tom got a little tongue-tied. He'd read both *Hand of Satan* and *The Devil's Maidens* more than once – and loved them. He wanted to begin his own novel while still at college: something epic, a band of supernatural adventurers travelling across continents. Something in the same vein as *The Devil Rides Out* or *The Satanist*. Wheatley knew how to spin a Homeric tale; an intricate tapestry of foreign locations and demonic cults.

The plane lurched and juddered suddenly and the 'fasten seatbelt' sign pinged on. Tom clicked his buckle hurriedly into place and drained the last of his whisky and ginger.

'Leon,' she began, 'you've been seeing this boy, Tom, for six months now. Why don't you bring him home to meet your mother? I don't have two heads!' Rosa Wilson handed her son a mug of coffee, gave him a wheedling smile. 'I think sometimes, darling, you're embarrassed by your old mum.'

'I know you don't have two heads, mum,' Leon said, taking a digestive from the packet on the kitchen table. 'It's just there's always so much course work to do, and we're only supposed to do our part-time jobs outside term. I promise I'll bring him down soon.'

'All right, darling.' Rosa pointed at him emphatically. 'I'll throw a party!'

'Why don't we just try a bit of lunch first?'

'He looks a handsome boy from the photo. You make a good-looking couple. I want to meet him. Soon.'

'Don't keep on,' Leon said good-humouredly. Rosa's opulent figure was squeezed into a long dress, lowcut at the neck. She had an amiable face, framed by neatly pressed hair. Her relaxed, often mischievous, manner belied the hardships and hurdles she'd had to overcome. Leon's father had worked as an engineer at a small tech company in north London. He died when Leon was just eight months old; a motorcycle accident at a busy junction on the North Circular. Rosa had been working for Midland Bank in Westward Hatch. She was still at the bank, although the name had changed to HSBC and the branch was Stratford now.

Rosa had raised Leon and his two older sisters, Cally and Sabena, on her own with a little help from Leon's Aunt Tashelle. Rosa never remarried. She'd never been interested though she hadn't been short of offers over the years. Her children were her focus; she wanted them to thrive and that's where all of her energy went.

'The girls are coming over on Christmas Eve, just in time for lunch,' she said. 'I thought we could go out for pizza. My diet's on hold until the New Year.'

The phone rang and Rosa went to answer it. She returned with a puckish grin. 'It's your boyfriend. I'll give you a little privacy.' She took her coffee and the packet of biscuits into the living room. Leon felt a familiar fluttering in his stomach as he picked up the receiver.

'Hey, how's things? Did you have a good trip?'

'The plane ride was a little bumpy,' Tom said. 'I hate flying in the winter.'

'You hate flying in the summer too.'

'I had to self-medicate. Quite a high dose.'

'I wish I'd been there to hold your hand. Preet texted to say she got to Manchester okay. She said Nancy went to see Sebastian in hospital. There's no change. Nancy says he looks terrible.'

'Poor Sebastian,' Tom said.

'How's it going with your folks?' Leon asked.

'My mother's got everyone geared up for the Big Catholic Christmas.'

'That bad, eh?'

'That bad. I've been posting bookstagram reviews to take my mind off it.'

'You should have spent Christmas with us. It's no distance from Cambridge and my mum's dying to meet you. I can't shut her up.'

'It's okay here and it's nice to see everybody. The whole family's been marshalled to welcome me home. I've only just managed to slip away to call you. I'll be summoned back to the front room any second.'

'Then I'd better tell you I love you, and let you go.'

'I love you too. I miss you.'

Tom turned to leave his bedroom; Tom's cousin, Róisín, all fidgety impulsiveness and freckles and tangled red hair, was standing in the doorway.

'Tom's got a girlfriend! Tom's got a girlfriend!' she chanted and bounded away before he could stop her.

His father was resting a large paw on the small girl's head as Tom came into the living room. He straightened up to his full height: six feet tall and wide as a Sherman tank. 'You're a dark horse, Thomas Donnelly,' he said, part reprimand, part proud statement. 'Why didn't you tell us you were courting? And what would the young lady's name be, now?'

vi

Christmas Eve. Preet's parents had lived in the same house for more than twenty years. It stood on the very edge – at one end of a mean little street. Around it, rows and rows of undifferentiated redbrick boxes in seemingly endless lines. And it was just as characterless as all the rest. Its front door opened directly onto the pavement. Its roof was black slate. A typical Rusholme house. The wind rattled bitterly through the streets and alleys. Pools of steely-grey water reflected the interminable greyness of the sky. Street lamps shone with a pale indifferent light. No blade of grass mitigated the starkness of the built environment. Manchester was now a post-industrial, reinvented Funkytown, full of arty coffeehouses, fine eateries, warehouses converted into smart apartments, cutting edge nightclubs, the Gay Village – Mad for it in Manchester! – but the cold grey rain still fell over these dryer Rusholme streets.

A small bedside lamp just about held the dark at bay. Beyond the foot of Preet's bed was a sea of shadow. She lay on top of the covers, her chest rising and falling gently as she dozed. Resting in her right hand was a book (of course): *Not After Midnight*, Daphne du Maurier. Her fingers twitched, as she loosened and tightened her grip in her sleep.

Preet is walking through Venice, hopelessly lost. It is nighttime and the narrow canals are badly lit. Tall houses rear up on either side of her. Moss-covered steps lead down to the water which gives off a faint fusty smell like rotten eggs. Long-hulled sàndoli tap against the canal walls in the dark. Preet is filled suddenly with an immense feeling of foreboding. A strangled cry comes from the other side of the canal. Now something is moving in the dark. It emerges from the arched doorway of a cellar but she can't quite make out what it is. It moves swiftly towards the water. And now she sees it properly: a child, probably about five or six years old; the girl is wearing a small waterproof coat with a pixie-hood. She jumps down into one of the moored sàndoli, then springs along the row. She pulls on the rope of the last boat, causing it to swing out across the canal towards the entrance of another cellar at the water's edge. For a split second the child almost falls. She looks up, her face caught in the glow of the lamplight. Preet catches her breath. It looks like Mahi, except it can't be. The face is twisted slightly out of shape like a rubber mask pulled by the hands of a spiteful child. Preet tries to cry out but, of course, no sound comes. Then Mahi-not-Mahi leaps across the water, landing

Preet sat up abruptly. She pushed her hair away from her face. Her underarms were damp with sweat. The door opened and her mother looked in anxiously.

'Are you all right?' she said. 'You were crying out. I thought you had an accident.'

'Just a bad dream,' Preet said. Her mother nodded and closed the door. Preet took a sip from the water glass by her bed. There was the du Maurier: *Don't Look Now*. She'd watched the film with Nancy, Tom, and Leon a few months ago. She'd been struck by just how beautiful Julie Christie was.

Preet had been to Venice with her parents when she was a teenager. She'd found it creepy, schizophrenic; the spectacle of the Grand Canal or St Mark's Square juxtaposed with the dark maze of dank little alleyways that criss-crossed the city. Venice was like a beautiful mask with a ruined face underneath. An involuntary shudder shook her body. Why was it so cold all of a sudden? She went to the wardrobe and took her nightdress off the coat hanger.

She had spent the last couple of weeks catching up with old school friends, going to obligatory family gatherings; avoiding Ravi, the medical student her mother harboured plans for her to marry. Three years of university provided a buffer against her mother's intentions and Preet had no plans to return home when her studies were finished. Cambridge was home now and that was where she intended to stay and find a husband of her own, if and when the time was right.

'You're too bloody stubborn,' her mother tutted, 'too

stubborn and independent-minded.' Plenty of truth in that. She was independent-minded and damned proud of it. She preferred relying on nobody but herself, making her own way in the world. Maybe she'd stay single forever. Wouldn't that put the cat among the pigeons? She might even end up marrying a woman – never say never – but for the time being, living in halls, with people her own age, people she liked, was exactly where she wanted to be. She loved her family but she couldn't help wishing she was back there, in Cambridge, right now.

The faintest scraping sounded at the window. She opened the curtains and saw a solitary red balloon pushing tentatively against the glass, as if trying to find a way in. There was something written on it but she couldn't make out what it said in the dark. The balloon juddered. Was it hissing now? Then, as if snatched by an invisible hand, it disappeared into the black.

chapter six

"In Tibet curling up with a good book is
invariably fatal."
THE SUNDIAL | SHIRLEY JACKSON

*'Du Maurier seems to relish highlighting
the city's seamier side,' said Freya.*

'Where do I start with this lot?' Judy asked, hands planted resolutely on her hips. The air in Freya's kitchen had a spicy sweetness to it and it looked like someone had thrown a grenade in there: impractical wooden worktops, faded and scratched, littered with open jars and tins; half-empty bottles of wine and packets of vegetables; unwashed pots, pans, colanders and wooden spoons piled up next to the draining board; houseplants and dog-eared cookery books in a shambolic huddle on the window sill. Freya was what Judy would call a 'chaotic' cook, the kind of person who produced the most delicious meals but left the kitchen looking like a bombsite in postwar London.

'Where do you start?' Freya said quizzically.

'You cooked lunch so I should wash up.'

'I won't hear of it,' Freya said. 'Let's leave it as it is for now. Kitchens have personalities. Mine's earthy and frenetic. I can't bear neat lines and scrubbed surfaces, all too anal. It's time for a little digestif.' She guided Judy back into the living room. Judy was suddenly thinking about Greta – Freya and Greta: chalk and cheese. With Greta, things had to be neatly cleared away, returned to their designated spots whenever they entertained. She was so used to keeping everything shipshape, it took quite an effort not to think about the mess in Freya's kitchen.

'How about a little *Matusalem*?' Freya said. 'It's Cuban rum. Deliciously sweet. Goes down very nicely.'

'I shouldn't,' Judy said, 'but I get the feeling you won't take no for an answer.'

'Say yes to everything. That was Quentin Crisp's motto.' Freya poured the rum while Judy settled onto the green chenille sofa draped with a thick woollen throw. It all felt so warm and cosy and safe, a taste of simple pleasure she'd been starved of for too long.

'Stretch out, relax,' Freya said as she placed Judy's glass on a small side table. 'What did you think of the *Frankenstein* movie?'

Judy laughed. 'I remember watching it as a teenager, BBC 2: the Saturday night Horror Double Bill. I was absolutely petrified. There's something sinister about those old black and white films.'

'It's probably because horror movies were in their infancy then. They were taken very seriously, made well, and audiences were genuinely frightened.'

'I must have been about twelve,' Judy said. 'My father had his own business, a working class boy made good, a dyed-in-the-wool Tory voter. We were the first family on our street to have a video recorder, a Grundig with those clunky Betamax tapes. My older brother used to video the Saturday night horrors and watch them the next morning. He teased me for being scared if I didn't watch them too, and I rose to the bait, of course. When all the other kids were at Sunday school, I was watching *Frankenstein*, *Dracula* and *The Wolf Man* – usually through my fingers.'

'We'll make a horror aficionado of you yet,' said Freya. 'Let me read you a bit now.'

Judy felt herself falling away, dissolving into a sweet *Matusalem* space. After sitting at Sebastian's bedside, they both needed to lift their spirits. She had to admit she'd had the most lovely afternoon. Freya was an accomplished host with an artless manner that made Judy more than a tad envious.

A deep oak bookshelf dominates one end of the living room. Freya is rummaging about, muttering to herself, chuckling as she plucks out a book bound in scarlet vellum. Judy rests her head lazily on a cushion; Freya perches at her feet. The pages rustle as Freya flips through the book then she begins to read, a traditional, old-school storyteller:

I trembled, and my heart failed within me; when, on looking up, I saw, by the light of the moon, the daemon at the casement. A ghastly grin wrinkled his lips as he gazed on me... he had followed me in my travels; he had loitered in forests, hid himself in caves... his countenance expressed the utmost extent of malice and treachery...

Despite the horror story, Judy had the oddest feeling of

serenity – simply, she realised, because she was here, close to Freya. It was a feeling she hadn't had in a long time. An image entered her mind: the first night at the Shirley Jackson Club; how nervous she'd been. She thought now of Eleanor, from the Hill House novel; a woman driven by forces beyond her control. She thought of Eleanor's final moments, her final words: 'I'm fine now. I was – happy... I don't want to go away from here.' Eleanor's last thoughts as she drove her car into a tree: 'I am really doing it, I am doing this all by myself, now, at last; this is me, I am really really really doing it by myself.'

...the utmost extent of malice and treachery...

And now, if only very briefly, Judy senses something hidden, watching her, watching all of them. She can feel the malevolent cunning of it; its hunger for human hopelessness and despair.

...malice... treachery... I don't want to go away from here... I don't want to go...

RED BALLOON

RED BALLOON

RED BALLOON

Freya has stopped reading. Her gaze is firm and tender. 'Are you okay? You were muttering to yourself.'

Judy sat up. 'I'm sorry, I was thinking about Hill House and Eleanor Vance, how lonely she was, how desperate for companionship. It struck a chord. You must think me very rude, drifting away while you're reading.'

'Not at all. We've both had a skinful!' Freya touched Judy's cheek lightly. Judy noticed the sudden light in Freya's eyes, dancing like fire on a winter's night.

Now they were kissing. Euphoric kisses. And Judy surrendered; let herself fall at last, realising she was no longer afraid.

Their lovemaking was long and unhurried, the gentlest exploration of one by the other – closer – hands and fingers on sensitive skin – closer – thighs, breasts, nipples.

– soft bellies –

– lifting belly –

touching and kissing; closer. Entangled, as the last of the daylight gave way to the relentless night.

Judy is woken up by the sound of rattling. The bedroom light is on. The unfamiliarity of the room wrong-foots her momentarily – odds and sods and trinkets everywhere; things that aren't hers, other memories gathered from another's life. Still only half-awake, she propped herself up awkwardly on one elbow. The unfamiliar mattress was just a little too soft; her back was stiff and her neck ached. Freya was lying on her side, speaking into her mobile phone. She put the phone back on the bedside table.

'That was the hospital,' she said. 'Sebastian's regained consciousness.'

'Thank goodness.'

'He's very weak but they say he'll be able to have visitors for a short time tomorrow.'

Judy's clothes were scattered across the bedroom floor where she'd let them fall. 'I should go.'

'You don't have to,' Freya said. 'You're very welcome to stay.' She paused. 'I don't have any expectations.'

'I think I should go all the same.' It wasn't that Judy felt guilty but staying for the night would have been the severing of something; a breaking of the invisible bond between her and Greta. And she wasn't ready to take that step. Freya kissed her gently on the forehead.

'Come with me tomorrow?'

Functional, faceless corridors, the smell of bleach and boiled cabbage, something cloying in the mix, very faintly: the bloody scent of clinical waste.

Hospitals made Judy uneasy; crowded with the old and infirm; a stark reminder of life's brevity. Holding cells for the dying, Greta always said. (Greta had died less than a week after the accident; so no dismal visits or drawn out vigil by her hospital bed.)

Sebastian's room seemed less austere in the daylight. A field of poppies danced under a clear sky in the painting she hadn't noticed the first time they visited. She watched Freya put a small vase of carnations on the pinewood nightstand. She wondered if all hospitals used the same furniture supplier. Sebastian smiled feebly. His right eye was bloodshot; his skin pale as milk.

'It's good to have you back,' Freya said. 'How are you feeling?'

'Sore,' he said. He half-lifted up his arm. His voice was barely audible. Freya sat down on the edge of the bed to hear him better and Sebastian grabbed her hand as if about to utter his dying words. 'You have to be careful,' he said, wrestling with speech, his chest rising and falling quickly under the bedclothes.

'Be careful?' Freya said. 'Why?'

'You're in danger. Everybody in danger. Pennywise. It came for me.'

'Try to stay calm. You've had a dreadful shock.'

'No!' He struggled to sit up, gripping Freya's wrist so tightly she almost cried out. 'It will come for you too. It sees us, it knows us.'

'You don't know what you're saying,' Freya said as evenly

as possible. 'You must try to be calm.'

Sebastian swallowed hard, trying to get the words out: 'I'm trying to warn you. You have to listen!' Sebastian was suffering from shock, or post traumatic stress, or the effects of concussion. Judy could see Freya's uneasiness growing. She stepped forward.

'Please, Sebastian, do try to lie quietly,' she said. 'It's important to get some rest.'

'No!' His body shook as he released his grip on Freya. He put a hand to his head as if to feel for some horror hidden inside. 'You have to listen. She came to me, don't you see? She really came!'

'What are you talking about?' Freya said. 'Who came to you?'

With one last almighty effort, Sebastian said: 'Shirley... Jack-son.' A long, hollow sigh and he slumped unconscious on the pillow.

'Good heavens,' Judy said. 'What on earth was all that about? He seemed almost —.' She rested a hand on Freya's shoulder. Freya stared straight ahead, frowning. 'Are you all right?' Judy asked.

'I went for lunch with Sebastian a while ago,' Freya said. 'He was very excited about the book he was writing. But there was something else he told me. He said that he was getting help from Shirley Jackson herself.'

Judy couldn't stifle a chuckle. 'That's preposterous. How could he possibly think such a thing?'

'I assumed he was channelling her in some way.'

'What does that mean?'

'Connecting with her on a spiritual plane.'

'You're not serious?'

'Of course I am.'

'He couldn't just dial the cosmic phone and talk to Shirley Jackson.'

'Anyone can commune with the dead if they have the knowledge. But maybe Sebastian did more than that. Maybe he brought her back into our world.'

'Oh, come on Freya. I don't care if she was the queen of horror. Authors don't come back from the dead.'

'According to Sebastian, they do.'

iii

'You look deep in thought, young man.' Judy had been looking forward to her pre-book-group americano at Bridges. Cambridge University had opened its doors again and so had the Shirley Jackson Club. Leon Wilson was one of the last people she expected to see. He should still be at St Benedict's with Tom, Preet and Nancy, or deep in a book of literary criticism at the English Faculty Library. She was a bit derailed by his sudden appearance; she had come to think of Bridges as her own private sanctuary. Greta used to tell her not to get too set in her ways, not to fixate about this or that particular spot but once Judy Miller developed a cosy ritual, she stuck to it. No deviations, no surprises.

She'd thought about missing the group this week. Freya had been distant after their visit to Sebastian. Judy asked if she'd done anything to offend her. Freya perked up instantly, dismissing the idea in her usual buoyant way; a little too buoyant this time, a stream of conciliatory words and smiles. Judy knew it was to do with the absurd idea that Sebastian had summoned up the ghost of Shirley Jackson. Judy liked Freya's pagan beliefs. It was all rather intriguing; a bit left field; off the beaten track; sweetly non-judgmental, no homophobia, no conservative family values. She'd have no problem tagging along to one of Freya's moots or sabbats – as an observer. Freya had told her there were eight festivals in the pagan year following the changing seasons – all finished off with cakes and ale. Sounded like fun. Judy liked the idea of a pantheon of gods and goddesses. Freya had talked about Diana, Cernunnos, Innana, Dionysus. Greta had lectured often enough on Greek and Roman belief systems. There was no harm in Wicca, Judy felt. It was just symbolism at the end of the day; none of it was real. And neither was calling authors back from the dead. Why couldn't Freya see how ridiculous that sounded?

The two of them had become regular companions, strolling along the Cam together, wrapped up against the biting Fenland wind that worried the trees and the water's surface. Their meet-ups were a regular fixture of life now, although they weren't 'an item' just yet. Judy needed to take things slowly, and she appreciated Freya's patience. Now Freya's strange mood had unbalanced things between them, and it bothered her. Maybe Freya needed her to believe in the supernatural, but Judy couldn't make that leap. So they walked, sometimes hand-in-hand, sometimes chatting idly, but ultimately saying very little.

'I haven't seen you in here before,' Judy continued as Leon looked up at her self-consciously (he thought she looked tired).

'Do you want to sit down?' he said.

(No, she didn't.)

'I don't want to disturb you,' she said, 'if you'd rather be alone?'

'Not at all,' Leon said, pushing out a chair. 'I'd be glad of the company.' Judy sat down. Leon was a pleasant boy and there was something on his mind. If he opened up, she could try to help. They started talking about *Not After Midnight*.

'Perhaps we'd better save all that for the group discussion,' Judy said. 'How was your Christmas?'

'I went home to my family in London. My mum's a force of nature so we were well-entertained and well-fed. What about you?'

'Just a quiet time,' Judy said carefully. 'Freya and I went to visit Sebastian on Boxing Day. He's still in quite a bad way, very confused. Concussion.' Let's hope Freya doesn't start bringing up the ghost of Shirley Jackson, she thought. 'And how's Tom? Did you spend any time together over the holiday?' He avoided her gaze, looked down at his half-empty coffee cup and his copy of *Norton's Anthology*.

'Tom's having a tough time of it,' he said. 'His cousin overheard him on the phone to me, put two and two together and came up with a girlfriend! Tom didn't deny it. Now he feels cowardly and ashamed for not telling the truth.'

'I take it his parents wouldn't be supportive?'

'They're very religious. And I wasn't very helpful. I said he should just tell them and to hell with it if they don't like it. He said it was easy for me. His upbringing was different. We got into a nasty fight.'

'It'll all blow over,' Judy said with a maternal smile. 'I was your age in the 1980s. We were all very careful back then. We had to be. It seems Tom's situation is a bit like that. I'm sure he'll work it out in his own time. And it's a sign of how strong your relationship is that you can have big disagreements and stay together.'

'I hope you're right.' Leon grinned weakly. Judy decided she really liked Leon. She was glad now she'd run into him. She liked the others too, Tom and Preet and Nancy; she liked them a lot.

'Are the others coming along tonight?'

'Tom and Preet are. Nancy has to help out at her parents' restaurant – for no pay, of course. They've got some leaving dos in, along with everything else, so it's all hands on deck.'

iv

Shirley Jackson Club Meeting:
Not After Midnight **– Daphne du Maurier.**
Heat rose valiantly from the convector heaters but the walls of the dank basement seemed to suck the warmth out of the air. Judy was glad of her thick cashmere jumper. She glanced at Tom surreptitiously; his face was stony, the face of a stranger. Freya threw Judy a contraband smile and Judy returned it. Perhaps life did begin at sixty. She poured herself a large glass of Viognier, hoping it would warm her up a bit while Freya handed round mince pies.

'I'm sure everybody's sick of these by now,' Freya said, 'but the sell-by date is today, so we might as well finish them off.' Judy helped Freya light the rest of the candles and they took their seats to discuss Daphne du Maurier's *Not After Midnight*. 'A collection of five long stories, as it says on the cover,' said Freya. 'The most famous one, of course, being *Don't Look Now*, the story of an English couple, John and Laura, on holiday in Venice while trying

121

to come to terms with the death of their daughter.'

'I thought that was the best story in the collection,' Leon said. 'The descriptions of Venice were so evocative. You felt you were there with them. The strange twin sisters were wonderfully drawn. And the idea that one of them was clairvoyant and could see the couple's dead daughter sitting next to them! Very eerie!'

'The murders happening in the city precincts,' said Judy, 'turned Venice into somewhere threatening and inhospitable rather than the beautiful and ancient tourist trap most people know. I got the sense that doom itself was stalking John and Laura, which of course it was.'

'Du Maurier seems to relish highlighting the city's seamier side,' said Freya, 'like the passage where she describes the water in the canal as limpid and pale and then the couple see a rat swimming in it.'

'The real twist, I think, isn't the ending,' said Tom, 'but the fact that John has second sight himself and doesn't realise it. He sees the twins and his wife in the boat on the canal and he sees his wife is distraught. He thinks it's real but it isn't. It's a vision of them after he's been murdered. Then a whole load of crazy events follow that one vision, a vision he completely misinterprets and which leads him to his death.'

'I think the ending was a clever and very nasty twist,' said Preet. 'The child in the pixie-hood that isn't a child at all but a woman with dwarfism who then kills John.'

'Nicely shocking in the film version too,' Tom added.

'You didn't tell us you'd watched the film,' Freya said, reprovingly.

'We saw it a while back, one of our horror movie nights.'

'You rotten lot!' Freya laughed. 'You should never watch the film before you've read the book!'

v

Nancy dropped freshly chopped cabbage into a large plastic bowl and wiped her forehead with her sleeve. She'd chopped and sliced and grated so much in the last couple of hours, the muscles and joints in her hands burned in protest. Since she was fifteen years old, she'd been called on to help out in the family restaurant at busy times.

'Fast', 'efficient' and 'easily plated' were her father's watchwords. True to those words, the Tokyo Palace had served good traditional Japanese food to the citizens of Cambridge for almost twenty years.

The kitchen was hot and hectic as usual, a hive of scurrying, white-coated activity. Orders were barked across the overcrowded space; pans slammed on gas rings, gas turned up; pots of steaming noodles poured into colanders. When Nancy first started working in the kitchen, she was only allowed to chop vegetables or boil rice and ramen. Later she was allowed to work on the meat and fish benches, preparing sushi or tonkatsu or yakitori, resisting – just – the temptation to sneak a mouthful each time she plated up a dish. Best of all, she liked to waitress. Freed from the steamy buzz of the kitchen (her father glowering at nervous members of the kitchen staff), she'd joke with customers, scribble down their orders, and pour out generous measures of wine, beer and spirits (a little too generous in her father's view). Tonight the restaurant was hosting two large parties and the Tokyo Palace was short staffed so it was all hands on deck, and organised mayhem at back of house.

'Nancy!' her father called, pointing a thumb at the recycling next to the back exit. She nodded in reply. Time for a break, anyway, she thought. She snatched up the recycling, kicked open the door and stepped out into the sharp night air.

The bins stood at the end of the narrow alley that ran parallel with the bars and restaurants of Mill Road. The passage was always poorly lit and smelled of rotting meat and veg; it was worst when the wind was in the wrong direction. The wind cut along the alley now, dropping greasy food wrappers at Nancy's feet. She must have walked out there a thousand times before but tonight something was different. Ill will was skulking in the shadows. It darted out from behind one of the commercial waste containers; a child, a girl in a red coat with a pixie-hood. What was she doing out here so late at night, and on her own? Pixie-hood stopped and looked at Nancy, her face obscure in the dismal lamplight at the end of the alley. There was something savage about this little girl. Why was she just standing there, looking at Nancy? Was she lost?

'Are you all right?' Nancy called.

Pixie-hood turned and headed down the alley, moving oddly, not like a child at all. Then she turned the corner and was gone.

Nancy first heard the word 'wiggins' in an episode of *Buffy the Vampire Slayer*. If Buffy Summers got the wiggins, you could be sure something particularly wicked was this way coming. Nancy had always felt wiggins described a special kind of misgiving, a very particular sensation of doom. Now, here in this godforsaken alley, Nancy definitely had the wiggins. She walked warily to the bins and quickly emptied the recycling before backing away swiftly down the passage. She didn't turn around until she was level with the restaurant's back door. Then she yanked it open and hurried inside.

chapter seven

"Abhorred monster! fiend thou art! the tortures of hell
are too mild a vengeance for thy crimes."
FRANKENSTEIN | MARY SHELLEY

*Pixie–hood runs past the church
into the shadows.*

i

Leon cleared his throat, 'Fancy coming for a drink at the Smokeworks?' he asked Preet. His tone had the forced provisionality of someone hoping for a 'no'. The boys were holding hands, fingers tightly interlocked – for Tom, a rare public display. But there was something else behind the gesture, something forced and self-conscious for Leon as well as Tom.

'I think I'll get back,' Preet said brightly, 'I've got that essay on Milton to finish.' She'd been putting the bloody thing off for too long. Endless diversions and subplots made *Paradise Lost* impossible to follow, and it was about

Christianity, hardly her theological strong suit. Tom and Leon clearly had things to talk about; their relationship had been noticeably strained of late. Preet walked with them as far as Bene't Street then she headed off with determined strides along Trumpington, hands deep in the pockets of her duffle coat.

She smiled as she reached Espresso Lane, her regular hangout with Nancy. The two of them were practically part of the furniture, always ordering the exact same thing: two flat whites and a ginger cake to share. She thought of their shopping trip yesterday, walking arm in arm along Sidney Street with their grocery lists and reusable eco-bags, laughing about boys they liked. Why were the best-looking boys always on other degree courses? Or gay? Or both?

Her hometown was rainy and cold but Fenland winters were much worse; the cold was a scimitar that sliced clean to the bone. The streets were bleak as a moonscape. The pitiless east wind swept in across carpets of flatland beyond the city limits and exhaled its profound cold into the ancient alleyways of the city. It gave her the same doleful feeling she got from being in love – when love is a desperate and disconsolate thing.

Now a fine sleet is falling, and she is glad of her cable-knit beanie, and she is thinking about the cold when she sees what looks like a child – a small girl – in a red coat with a pixie-hood (of course). The child stumbles and falls and a sharp little wail rings out in the raw night air. Then the girl scrambles to her feet, looking over her shoulder, turns, and runs with faltering steps along the middle of the road.

Preet is reminded of her nightmare: Mahi and Venice;

Mahi alone, Mahi frightened, Mahi running. She had been so affected by the dream, she posted about it on her bookstagram. Mahi had been wearing the same red coat; could the dream have been a presentiment of something actual? Was Preet meant to help the child? Had an authentic presentiment been somehow coloured and distorted by the du Maurier? (Second sight and premonition are essential to the du Maurier story.) The girl must have hurt herself when she fell. Most children would lie there and cry, waiting for mother or father to wrap comforting arms around them, kiss it all better. But this child jumped up again and ran away. She was afraid of something or someone, and alone (like Mahi). Preet runs after the child in the freezing night. When she looks back the way the child had come, she sees a man in dark clothes running towards them along Botolph Lane. Pixie-hood runs past the church into the shadows of Little St Mary's Lane. Preet hears the child's sobs and watches her turn and turn again, this time past the weathered railings that mark the boundary of the churchyard. Then she halts suddenly in front of the great arched gateway to Peterhouse College.

'It's all right,' Preet says quietly, holding out her hands. 'No one is going to hurt you.' The small figure remains stock-still, her back to Preet. The man's footfalls are rapid and closer now. 'Please let me help you,' Preet says, softly. 'Why are you running away?' Pixie-hood does not turn around. Instead, a slight, sudden movement of the child's right arm and something drops into her hand. She turns sharply and the pixie-hood falls to her shoulders. The small figure is no child, but a dwarf (of course), her large head framed with matted strands of grey hair. Her face is immensely wrinkled, ancient, and her eyes are deepest black. She isn't sobbing now, but grinning and nodding her head slyly as she raises her right hand. The knife punctures Preet's throat with unbelievable ease. It slices through the windpipe as if through kalamari until its glinting point juts obscenely from the back of Preet's neck. She collapses awkwardly against the railings, feeling no pain at all, only the most intense surprise. I have been stabbed with a knife, she thinks simply to herself as she curls her fingers round the handle. It is as if her whole body is suspended from the knife's edge. The droplets of blood, already trickling from her neck, will become a scarlet tide if she withdraws the blade. Pixie-hood is babbling something, jumping up and down ecstatically. Preet hears the man's pursuing footsteps almost upon her as the world turns to darkness and all she can think is, No, please. I can't die like this.

ii

An array of colourful cocktails passed into eager hands across the bar; elbows resting on high wooden tabletops; the buzz of carefree chatter. Leon taps the card reader the barman offers him, and glances back at Tom perched on a brown leather couch by the window. Tom looks a little lost; the 'girlfriend' thing with his family has really got to him. Leon couldn't help thinking how happy they'd been last summer; scrabbling the money together for a getaway in Sitges; dancing until closing time at Man Bar; walking along *Carrer de Joan Tarrida* under a sea of rainbow flags; anonymity and freedom, strangers in a strange land.

They soon found *Playa de la Bassa Rodona*, alive with

bronzed and sculpted male bodies, designer sunglasses and clinging speedos. But there was only one man Leon wanted to gaze at: Tom was lean and lovely and Leon's entirely for seven glorious days.

They made love in the cemetery above *Playa de las Balmins* at midnight, when else? The tumbledown headstones, the warm, dry earth, the thrum-thrumming of the cicadas. As he slid down onto Tom in the sultry dark, taking him in, Leon felt nothing could hurt them.

Now, the whole 'girlfriend' lie was hurting them both. Leon placed two dirty martinis on the low table in front of Tom. 'Got a new message?'

'My brother Sean. He went to mum and dad's last night. Mum keeps going on about how she wants to come over to Cambridge... and meet my girlfriend.'

'Put her off.'

'She can be very persistent.'

'She'll give up eventually.'

'No. She won't.'

'You could always tell her you've split up.'

'She'll just start lining up girls back home.'

'So don't go home.' Leon squeezed Tom's thigh reassuringly. 'It's not as if they live down the road. And it's not as if they found out the 'awful truth' about you.'

Tom offered up a watery smile. 'I thought you wanted me to come out?' he said.

'I do because I think you'll be more comfortable in your own skin. I want you to be happy and free to be you without having to look over your shoulder. But you have to do it in your own time.'

'You've changed your tune.'

'Maybe I've been pushing you for the wrong reasons. I

thought you could do things the same way I did, but your situation is completely different. You don't have a mother who's an incorrigible diva and delighted to have a gay child!'

Tom laughed in spite of himself.

'And you know what a Radical Faery I can be.'

'You should see if they'll give you a membership card.'

'It'll all work out in the end. Honestly it will.'

'You're right about coming out,' Tom said. 'I should bite the bullet, stop being such a yellow belly.' He inched a little closer to Leon and took his hand. 'I think we should drink up, and go home...'

The sleet is falling more decisively now, pitter-pattering against the bedroom window like so much wet sand falling.

The two young men pull up the bedclothes against the cold, breath on breath, skin on skin; intensity of feeling intense enough to slow the apparent passage of time. Sensitive, eager fingertips brush skin to skin; completeness of feeling; a kiss; another; another. They twist against each other, warm as fresh bread. Leon curls his legs around Tom, holding him momentarily, inviting him, willingly pregnable. Tom is more than hungry, a starving man now, as he holds Leon's shoulders and gently pushes inside him, moving with soft, tender insistence. They become one another, joyously permeable, souls migrating across the divide of their flesh as they crest together.

Leon's head is on Tom's chest, ears filled with the beating of Tom's heart. Something else sounds in the distance, moving closer. Footfalls on the stairs? The sound ceases abruptly and a shadow breaks the line of light under the door. Then the hard, adamant banging of a fist against wood. Tom moans hazily. The door is rattling in its frame; the banging from the other side isn't going to stop. Leon tosses back the covers.

'Okay! Okay! Just a minute!' The banging ceases. He pulls on his jeans and opens the door, squinting under the landing's bright lights. Nancy is standing in her dressing gown; beside her, a uniformed policewoman. Nancy is fighting back tears. 'What's going on?' Leon says.

'The police are here,' Nancy says superfluously. 'It's Preet. She's dead. Somebody killed her.'

iii

The police constable glanced at Judy as he walked past carrying a sheaf of papers. His face was lean and young. He's way too young to be out on the streets chasing villains, Judy thought. She shifted her weight on the mean little plastic chair. Her left buttock was numb. The whole place was in need of a good lick of paint and a tidy-up. The corkboard opposite was choked with helpline numbers and posters about everything from domestic abuse to knife crime. Just a short time ago Preet had been chatting merrily away about Daphne du Maurier, her supervision work on Milton, her on-off holiday job at Heffers. Now she was laid out on a slab behind a gunmetal door. Her friends were too distressed to identify the body. Freya suggested she and Judy do it.

At least her parents wouldn't have to see her drawn out from a cold cabinet. Better to see her at the undertakers. The morticians would do everything they could to make her look peaceful, to mask the awful fact of her death. Judy had thought she'd be able to go into the mortuary, support

135

Freya, but in the end she couldn't do it. The memory of Greta's lifeless body was too raw, the terrible absence of the lovely conscious thing who had been her wife, had loved her, had faced adversity with her. She remembered wondering where that person could have gone. She still hadn't got over that day. She never would.

The door opened and Freya came out, followed by Inspector Sorensen. Freya's face bore no expression. She looked blankly at Judy and Judy put her arms around her.

'Who could have done this?' Judy said to the Inspector.

'As far as we know,' Sorensen said, 'it seems Miss Chanda was trying to catch up with an unaccompanied child. According to our witness, the child was running in the middle of the road. He was concerned she might get knocked down so he ran after her. At Trumpington Street, he saw the girl fall and Miss Chanda run to her aid. They both disappeared into Little St Mary's Lane. When the man finally caught up with them, the child was gone and Miss Chanda had been fatally wounded with a knife.'

Judy winced. 'What about the child?' Judy said 'Have you found her? Was she harmed?'

'She hasn't been located yet,' Sorensen cleared her throat, 'but we've put out an APB for a girl in a pixie-hood.'

'A girl in a pixie-hood?' Freya repeated. 'We've just been reading *Don't Look Now* at our book club.'

'I'm not sure I'm following,' said Sorensen.

'It's a story by Daphne du Maurier. A girl in a pixie-hood kills someone with a knife. But it turns out it isn't a girl at all but a woman with dwarfism.'

'You think somebody read the book and re-enacted the killing?'

'It does seem rather coincidental,' Freya said.

'Who outside your book group knew you were reading this story?'

'There's Alta who works full time in the shop but she isn't a member of the Shirley Jackson Club.'

'Shirley Jackson?'

'The name of our book group. We read horror fiction – Shirley Jackson was a famous horror writer.'

'So apart from your employee, nobody else knew you were reading this book?'

'We post our reading list on the Persephone's website, also on our socials. Anybody who cared to look would have known.'

Judy put her hand on Freya's shoulder, 'Do you really think somebody read *Don't Look Now* and set out to kill Preet in the same way? It sounds quite elaborate, doesn't it?'

Sorensen closed her notebook. 'I agree, it does seem a little outlandish but we can't rule anything out at this stage.'

Sorensen walked them down the corridor. 'I'm going to need a statement from each of you and the other members of the Sally Jackson Club.'

Freya frowned: '*Shirley*, Inspector.'

iv

The comforting burble of espresso machines, ground coffee steaming in paper cups, busy baristas in narrow galleys before long queues of people; the city of Cambridge was wide awake and impatient for its morning fix. Outside the sky was bright and colourless, the pavements full; students wrapped in thick jackets and scarves cycling to lectures on the other side of town; commuters pouring out of buses, same old same old. (How much longer to the weekend?) Alta was just putting the vacuum cleaner away when Judy and Freya arrived. Vacuuming, dusting, putting disordered books back in their rightful places – these were the mundane jobs people rarely associated with running a bookshop. But Freya wouldn't have it any other way; it was so magical being alone here, early in the morning, or late at night, with just shelves and shelves of books for company; her own little kingdom.

Judy always found Alta wonderfully full of laughter; she seemed to come at life with unparalleled ease. Judy supposed some of that was down to her Caribbean roots, and she envied her those roots. But today Alta's face bore no warm and effortless smile. She was a contradiction of half-made gestures, talking nervously about last night's gruesome knife attack: a young woman, and right in the centre of Cambridge. (Alta herself didn't live more than a couple of minutes walk from Little St Mary's Lane.) When Freya broke it to her that the victim was Preet, she pressed her hand to her mouth and threw back her head, sobbing inconsolably. Freya sent her home; Persephone's would be closed today as a mark of respect.

Freya's office was a tiny cupboard of a room, and a hopelessly jumbled mess: UPS delivery boxes, stacks of papers, towers of books. She made two mugs of strong black coffee and produced a half-empty bottle of Glenmorangie from the bottom drawer of a filing cabinet that leaned rather than stood against the wall. She added a generous dash of whisky to each mug then handed one to Judy. 'To steady the nerves,' she said. Judy wasn't sure she could drink whisky so early in the day. She followed Freya into the basement where the Shirley Jackson Club had met the night before. For a while, neither of them could find any words and Judy stared numbly at the chair Preet usually sat in. Always the same chair. Every single week. I wonder why she chose that particular one? Maybe there wasn't a reason, she thought inanely, just force of habit. What strange creatures human beings are. Freya's voice snapped her back.

'Something really bizarre is going on,' she said.

'The similarity with the du Maurier story? Coincidence,' Judy said hopefully.

'You didn't see Preet's body.'

'I'm sorry, I just couldn't face it. I thought I could but I-'

'That's not what I mean. You didn't see the wound.' Freya picked up her copy of *Not After Midnight*. She flipped through the pages to the closing lines of *Don't Look Now*. She read: '...he saw the child... It was the same little girl with the pixie-hood... The child struggled to her feet and stood before him, the pixie-hood falling from her head on to the floor... It was not a child at all but a little thick-set woman dwarf... The creature fumbled in her sleeve, drawing a knife... she threw it at him... piercing his throat...' Freya paused decisively and closed the book.

'I'm still not sure...' Judy told her.

'Preet had a knife wound to the throat.'

Judy shivered.

'And the child, or what seemed like a child, wearing a pixie-hood?' Freya asked.

'You really do believe someone killed Preet in the same

way?'

'Not someone,' Freya said. 'Something.'

'Something?' Judy tried to keep her tone as even as she could. 'Come on, Freya, this is real life not one of Sebastian's novels.'

'How do you explain it, then?'

'Any number of ways.'

'Really? Pick one.'

v

The only house on the street with a slate grey front door; the only house with a lion's head door knocker, the brass handle and lion's head tarnished a muddy greenish-brown; white paint tired and flaking off long-neglected window frames; maybe Sebastian really needed this new book of his to be a success. Maybe that was why he'd been so reckless. Freya lost track of how long she'd been standing on the other side of the road, looking at the house. Damn it, she thought, why hadn't he come to me first? I would have made sure he took the right precautions. His unknown attacker was loosed on the world. Now it had claimed a second victim.

Sebastian had started to regain consciousness properly about a fortnight ago. He had been moved to a respite clinic to recuperate and now, although still weak, he was well enough to return to his own home at last with a nurse to look after him a few hours a day. Freya's mind was full of questions as she lifted the heavy brass knocker. She was sure the nurse would answer but, if she didn't, Freya had a set of keys (she watered Sebastian's plants whenever he was away). There was no answer. She was about to reach

140

into the pocket of her teddy coat when she heard footsteps clicking in the hallway. The door opened decisively to reveal a small, gaunt woman with grey hair pulled back into a severe bun. She was wearing a knee-length black dress with white collar and cuffs like an old-fashioned housemaid. She looked Freya up and down dubiously with the air of someone sizing up a door-to-door salesman.

'Can I help you?'

'I'm here to see Sebastian.'

'You are?'

'Freya Bancroft.' Freya decided she didn't like the woman's tone, or anything else about her for that matter.

'Follow me.'

'I was expecting someone in a nurse's uniform,' Freya said as she followed the woman to the foot of the stairs. The woman stopped abruptly.

'I am Sebastian's sister, Theodora.'

'Pleased to meet you.'

Theodora didn't accept the hand Freya offered but folded her arms instead.

'I didn't know Sebastian had a sister.'

'He's upstairs,' Theodora said coolly. 'Second on the left when you get to the top.' Then she stepped into the living room and closed the door behind her.

Sebastian was lying limply on a low oak bed. The patchwork quilt had seen better days. He was asleep, breathing shallowly. Freya pulled up a chair and took hold of his hand. His eyes drifted open and he tried to sit up but she shook her head. 'Lie back and rest.'

'Dreams,' he said in little more than a whisper, 'I've had the most terrible dreams, terrible nightmares.'

'Sebastian,' Freya said, 'I have to ask you something.'

She tried to appear relaxed; she didn't want to agitate him. 'The night you summoned Shirley Jackson...'

'You believe me?'

'Of course I do.' She leaned closer and, as she did so, a little zephyr of fear touched the back of her neck; she had the strangest sense that Theodora had crept up the stairs behind her and was listening at the door. 'How did you do it? How did you summon her?'

'Why?' he said. 'What's happened?' He paused, searching her face. 'Something's happened, hasn't it? I can tell from your face.' Freya was silent for a moment, choosing her next words carefully.

'Something did happen,' she told him. 'Someone from the group had a strange encounter. I can't tell you any more but, please Sebastian, how did you summon Shirley Jackson?'

'The mirror,' he hissed, 'through the mirror.'

'I see.' Freya raised her eyebrows, piecing things together. 'The mirror allowed you a psychic connection with Shirley Jackson. It acted as a *pyschomanteum.*'

Sebastian was searching her face more intently now.

'It attacked someone else didn't it?' Sebastian said. 'The clown.'

'No, not the clown. Where's the mirror now?' Freya said. But it was no good, Sebastian was already exhausted; he had lapsed back into unconsciousness.

'There's something of mine here,' Freya said to Theodora. 'Sebastian was looking after it for me. It is a rather ornate mirror. It belonged to a favourite author of mine. I'd like to take it with me, if I may?'

'I don't know anything about a mirror,' Theodora said, her lips pressed into a thin, pale line.

'If you do happen upon it, will you call me, please?'
Freya hunted through her bag for a pen and paper.

'There's no mirror here,' Theodora told her. 'Good day to you, Miss Bancroft.'

The woman who had called herself Theodora watched from an upstairs window until Freya turned and disappeared at the end of the street. She straightened up and directed her gaze towards Sebastian's bedroom. She stood in the doorway and regarded the old author, his chest rising and falling unevenly, his breathing laboured. As she approached the bed, he opened his eyes.

'And how is the patient?' she asked, betraying no hint of compassion.

'Tired, really quite tired. And really quite thirsty. Might I get a cup of tea?'

'I hope you haven't been overtaxing yourself, kiddo, chatting with that woman. No more visitors for you, I think.'

Sebastian tried to push himself up against his pillows. 'Please, nurse,' he said. 'I am really thirsty. Might I get some tea?'

'Water's good enough for you,' she said, filling the glass on his bedside table from a heavy pewter jug. 'That's all you need. And no more talking. To anyone. Remember, Nurse Morgen knows best.'

'Nurse, please,' Sebastian cried out to her as she glided through the door, pulling it closed behind her. 'Come back. Nurse Morgen, please!'

On the other side of the city, Tom Donnelly was pouring hot water into two mugs, stirring tea bags and adding milk. He sat down in a tattered armchair and pressed the record and play buttons on an old Nuvox tape recorder. The elderly gentleman opposite him raised the mug to his lips, his sightless eyes staring blankly ahead. His head moved almost imperceptibly as the tape machine clicked and whirred. Tom took up the small microphone and began speaking: 'Interview with Arthur Barker, resident of Cambridge, 96 years of age.'

Tom had seen a flyer for the LGBT+ Oral Histories project tied to a railing outside Great St Mary's Church. It was organised by a network of elderly gays and lesbians as a way to document and preserve the lives of queer Cambridge residents. They'd wanted young people to conduct the interviews and Tom had been quick to volunteer. He really needed to keep himself occupied every waking hour; anything to take his mind off what had happened to Preet.

'What was your first gay experience?' Tom asked, holding the microphone towards Arthur.

'The end of the Second World War,' Arthur said, fingers tapping softly on the armrest of his chair. 'An American soldier staying with my parents. Howard was his name. He had the most beautiful olive skin. He came from California, a lovely drawling accent like late sunshine.'

'How old was he?'

'Twenty-two. I was nearly seventeen. My parents were out for the day on a visit to London for something or other. Howard and I went for a walk. He asked me if I'd ever had a girlfriend. I said 'no'. He said he hadn't either;

he'd never been interested in any woman. We'd taken a small picnic and we sat on the grass at the top of Constitution Hill looking down over the valley. I remember the colours of the fields that day as if it were yesterday. Then he put an arm around me, just looked at me, searching I suppose for any hint of shock or rejection. And soon we were kissing. It was a very warm day. I remember thinking this was the start of something, the start of happiness, of the rest of life.'

'Were you worried someone might find out?'

'Of course: it was illegal then. We had to be very careful but I also knew I had to be true to myself. I wasn't going to get married, ruin the life of some poor girl as well as my own. Howard went back to America about a week or so after. We had some lovely, stolen hours together, then he was gone. Soon after that, like so many other homosexual men, I set off for London.'

'Do you regret being young back then when it was more difficult for gay men?' Tom asked.

'It's much easier for young people these days,' Arthur said with a rueful smile, 'but I can't say I regret my time. I found other men in London. And, as I said, I had to live my life my own way, not by anybody else's rules. It must be so much easier for you young people now, now that you're all *out and proud*.'

Tom flushed; this man had been brave in such difficult, hostile times. 'Not everyone is accepting nowadays,' Tom said. 'My family are very conservative.'

'Then you must find yourself another.'

chapter eight

"He felt himself held, unable to move, an impending sense of doom, of tragedy, came upon him."
DON'T LOOK NOW | DAPHNE DU MAURIER

*The balloon twisted free
and mounted into the Stygian sky.*

i

Freya had suggested they meet at her house instead of the bookshop. Everyone agreed. Tonight would be the first time they were all together since Preet's murder. No one wanted to be in the old room with Preet not there. It still felt horribly unreal that Preet was gone. They'd discussed giving up the group entirely but Nancy said Preet wouldn't want that (even though she, Tom and Leon had given up on horror movie night because it was too painful).

Tom scanned his shelves for this week's book: *The Bloody Chamber* by Angela Carter. His eye caught *The Rats* instead. James Herbert was one of his favourite horror writers. He loved the grittiness of Herbert's stories and his undisguised criticism of society which threw so many of its most vulnerable members to the wolves. Or in this case, to the giant disease-ridden rats.

Preet had come across the first edition in a clearance sale. Whoever priced up the books was no horror buff: this copy was signed by the author and was worth a small fortune. She bought it for Tom, knowing he was an ardent Herbert fan. Tom touched the book gently. Yes, it was a collector's item. Yes, he'd never part with it, especially now.

He opened the book at random and began to read: 'The rat gave out a piercing shriek and loosened the grip on his leg. Its neck was trapped between the door and frame but still it thrashed around wildly, its eyes glazed and its mouth frothing'. Herbert always made him feel he was there in the thick of it, cornered and in terrible danger alongside the characters on the page. He put the book back, and sighed.

There was his copy of *The Bloody Chamber*; he took it down from the shelf.

He found Nancy in Preet's old room. 'We'd always have a quick chat before going to the group, share some thoughts about this week's book, usually over a coffee and a ginger biscuit.'

'Preet did love a ginger biscuit,' Tom said.

'She always reckoned they were too spicy to make you fat,' Nancy said. 'God knows where she got that idea from.'

'Wishful thinking.'

They stood in silence for a little while. The mattress was propped up against the wall. The shelves had been stripped of books. The desk under the window had one drawer half open, also empty. Everything was empty. They heard Leon out on the landing. 'Come on,' Nancy sighed, 'let's go and make her proud with our insightful analysis of the mighty Angela Carter.'

The three students made their way towards the lofty iron gates of St Benedict's. The college grounds were enclosed within high walls obscured by a well established line of fir trees. The dark trees gave the impression of cutting St Benedict's off from the world outside. The night was sharp again; a steady wind sighed through the swaying branches. Leon was regaling Nancy with the wonders of beef patties. Tom trailed a little way behind, lost in thought. The secret, Leon explained, was Aunt Tashelle's magic ingredient: hot pepper sauce, very, very hot pepper sauce.

Something moved at the base of the tree line; darting and scurrying, large and dark, about the size of a dog. Tom stopped to look.

As if sensing him, the dog-thing also stops and stares back at him. Its eyes are yellow in the moonlight. It rears up on its hind legs. And just as suddenly, it's gone.

Then Leon is calling back: 'Hey, Tom, you okay?'

'I thought I saw something.'

'Like what?'

'I can't be sure, but it looked like a rat.'

ii

Five glasses – a solemn toast: 'To absent friends.'

'Angela Carter was one of her favourite writers,' Nancy said quietly. 'I'm glad we're talking about one of her books tonight.'

'*The Bloody Chamber* is quite a collection,' Freya said

gently. 'Carter said that every fairy story, sitting on a nursery shelf was a bomb – and if you turn it right, it will blow up. In *The Bloody Chamber* she gives us her version of ten traditional fairy tales. Even in their traditional forms, fairy tales are powerful things – they shape our view of the world from a very young age. But in Carter's retellings, they show us something else – that there's an ice-cold heart dripping with blood at the core of all fairy stories.'

'Philip Pullman said fairy tales were too easy for children and too difficult for adults,' Tom offered.

'*The Company of Wolves* was my favourite,' said Leon.

'Mine too,' said Tom.

'Let me guess,' Freya said, 'you've seen the film?'

'Yes,' said Tom, 'but a very long time ago. It's quite difficult to get hold of these days.'

'*The Company of Wolves* is a standout story,' Freya said. 'Little Red Riding Hood is seduced by the wolf. It's certainly the sexiest of the stories in the collection, and the closest of all to out-and-out horror.'

'I like the way the girl turns the tables on the wolf man,' Nancy said, 'stripping and getting into bed with him at the end of the story rather than being eaten. It's animalistic and carnal.'

Freya nodded, 'She definitely asserts her own sexuality, and engages with her bestial nature just as much as he does.'

'She was nobody's meat,' said Leon, quoting from the text. 'I liked the other references to lycanthropy: the man who leaves his wife on their wedding night and is presumed dead. When she remarries, he returns, flies into a rage, and becomes a wolf again. The huntsmen kill him, and his human form reappears beneath the wolf's skin. Terrific!'

'The worst wolves are hairy on the inside,' Freya grinned. 'God, I love Angela Carter. She puts gender and sexuality centre stage with powerful women characters who are smart and hungry, more than a match for the men, or wolves, they encounter.' She turned to Judy. 'What do you think?'

Judy shifted a little uncomfortably. Her mind had been elsewhere. 'The wolves don't seem particularly happy,' she said, 'and I wonder if that's a comment on men in general and men's sexual appetite. The story seems to say we can keep the wolves at bay by excluding them. They are painfully thin, their ribs showing through from starvation. Perhaps being an infernal carnivore has its disadvantages. Perhaps it's all sex. They can't get enough. They're wasting away for want of it. Perhaps all men are starving in that department.' Judy stopped talking and blushed.

'Hmmm... interesting.'

iii

It had been staring at him sullenly for a few days now, growing larger and larger, overflowing its basket until more than half of it rested messily on the floor. Tom realised he had to do something about it; take it in hand, show it who's boss. He wrestled the heap of laundry into a large plastic sack, scooped up a pack of washing capsules and headed outside to the laundry block. Most of the other students were out at formals so no light was showing from their windows to light the way. Tonight the moon was half-obscured, riding a dirty-grey bank of cloud. Tom

153

hadn't felt like dinner; his stomach was griping again with IBS brought on by the awfulness of Preet's death, by the stress of living a lie whenever he went home or talked to his mother on the phone; by life itself. He tapped the torch on his mobile. The beam was blueish, cold, and he felt a familiar tugging in the pit of his stomach; not IBS but a diffuse dread; dread with no object. He couldn't explain why he felt this way, but he was pleased to see the laundry block lit up, casting a pool of warm light that defeated the little bit of night around it. A red balloon stood out in the light, caught on the step by the door. It was freezing to the touch; almost tore the skin from Tom's fingers. When he snatched his hand back from the unexpected cold, the balloon twisted free and mounted into the Stygian sky.

Tom dumped his laundry in front of one of the washers. The lights flickered briefly, seemed to rally for a moment, then died. 'Shit,' he muttered. He tried the button on the washer and a row of green lights appeared – no power cut, then. He turned his torch back on against this new dark and propped the phone next to him on the concrete floor. In the torchlight, his hands looked blue-white like a cadaver's. There'll be spare light bulbs at the porter's lodge, he thought, I'll put the wash on then go and ask for one. But Tom didn't relish the idea because Bob Stahlman was on duty tonight; a crotchety old toad who wouldn't rush to help someone if they were choking to death. Tom reckoned it might be easier just to do the washing by torchlight.

He sorted the laundry into whites and coloureds. It struck him this was just how he was living his life now: separating two versions of himself: *Tom with Leon* (the life and times of the real Tom Donnelly); *Tom with his family* (the great big lie). He decided there and then, separating red socks from white briefs, that he was going to do it – he was going to tell his parents he was gay. If they never spoke to him again, that would be their choice. He'd always been a cuckoo in the nest; the strange, introspective boy with his nose in a book, no interest in girls; the family's first Cambridge undergraduate, made outsider through no fault of his own by his innate cleverness.

Leon was his family now; Leon and Nancy and his friends at college, and Freya and Judy too. Your true family was the one you chose for yourself, the people who really cared about you, your found family, your tribe.

This little reverie was interrupted by something scratching at the door. He stood stock still and listened: now he heard *more than one something* scratching at the door. The skitch-skitch-skitch was coming from all directions. At the window, three large rats appeared in the sudden light from the night-riding moon and more brownish shapes were gathering behind them. The skitch-skitch-skitch was loudest at the base of the door. Tom backed slowly away, caught his phone with the heel of his shoe and it spun across the floor, disappearing under one of the dryers.

'Shit!'

He flattened himself against the floor, peering into the narrow space; managed to slide his arm in as far as the elbow. It was tight, very tight. The tips of his fingers touched the smooth edge of the phone, but he couldn't get any purchase. His efforts only nudged it further away. Then the torch went out and in the dark his imagination took over. *The metal of the dryer was compressing his arm. Skin and bone turned cuttlefish-white as the blood was cut off.*

Now something was tugging at the tips of his fingers, gently at first then, tearing the skin, eating away at his trapped limb. Stop it, he thought, and yanked his arm out from underneath the dryer, scraping the skin from his knuckles along the way, yelping like an wounded dog. Before he could get to his feet, the rat came for him, skittering at terrific speed across the floor, sinking the little razors of its teeth into his neck. He managed to get hold of it by the scruff but it was already too late and he felt a sticky warmth trickling from his neck to his chest. He beat the rat's skull against the dryer, sickened by the sound of the skull bone knocking against metal. The rat's outraged squealing gave way to gurgling as blood filled its gullet. Its body hung limply from Tom's bloody hands and he dropped the ragged mess onto the floor.

Then his leg was bitten. He prised the rat free but a length of greasy white tendon tore away with it. He dispatched this rat as swiftly as the first but the burning sensation in his injured leg was intolerable; blood from the wound was already pooling on the floor.

The laundry door juddered like an epileptic. Tom could hear the rats beating themselves against it. It was only a matter of time before it would break open. He hobbled towards it, working against the terrible pain in his leg but the door gave way before he could reach it and the rats poured in like so much filthy, black water. Tom looked around for something, anything, to use as a weapon. A copy of the *Cambridge News*, rolled tightly, made a serviceable baton. He used it to defend his face but the vermin were insatiable, making instinctively for his throat, gorging themselves on the soft under-flesh in that most vulnerable of places. His screams faltered then stopped.

Silence.

Nothing remained of Tom Donnelly but a skull picked clean; tooth and bone; an oily mess of viscera. The hell-born creatures inundated the laundry, trailing blood and entrails, massing against the windows until, with an almighty shattering, the glass exploded and the rats surged over the college lawns and into the trees.

iv

Freya jabbed an emphatic finger at the newspaper article:

STUDENT DEATH LINKED TO RAT INFESTATION. *Cambridge City Council has come under intense pressure to tackle a dangerous rat infestation after a student was found dead last night. St Benedict's College student Tom Donnelly, 20, was killed in an unprecedented attack yesterday evening. Mr Donnelly was mauled to death at around 8pm in the college grounds. 'I heard screams coming from the direction of the halls and then the sound of glass smashing,' said duty porter, Robert Stahlman, 64. 'When I came out of the porter's lodge, I couldn't believe what I saw. There were hundreds of very large rats, a plague of 'em, running across the lawn to the trees. I went into the laundry room and found the body, chewed to pieces. It was so badly injured, I couldn't tell who it was.' Police officers were called to the scene but could find no trace of the killer rats. The bizarre attack comes just weeks after another St Benedict's student, Preet Chanda, was murdered in the city centre. The two incidents have prompted some to label this 'the curse of St Benedicts'.*

'D'you see?' Freya said.

'I'm afraid I don't,' said Judy blankly, her face white as ashes.

'It's *The Rats*!'

'The rats?'

'James Herbert. People were mauled to death in that novel by huge black rats.'

'I'm aware of that, Freya. It's a revolting story.'

Freya paced up and down like a professor expounding a revolutionary theory. 'This is conclusive proof. Inspector Sorensen is denying any connection between Preet's murder and Tom's death, and she's wrong.'

'You spoke to her about this?' Judy couldn't keep the incredulity out of her voice. Freya must be in shock; it was the only explanation. Judy imagined Freya hectoring the inspector with her supernatural conspiracy theories.

'Yes, absolutely,' Freya continued, dabbing her nose with a handkerchief. 'But she says it's an environmental matter, not the police's jurisdiction.'

'She sounds right about that. They say in London you're never more than six feet away from a rat.'

'We're not talking about a rat, we're talking about hundreds of them, we're talking about *The Rats*. First the killer in the pixie-hood, now the rats. Something beyond our understanding, something darkly malevolent is killing members of our book group, aping the horror books we've been reading.'

'No, Freya. That simply can't be true. You're not thinking clearly. It could just be coincidence, or there's a psychopath on the loose.'

'No, it isn't that!'

'All right, then,' Judy said, she didn't want to get into a

fight, 'just supposing there is some kind of strange thing going on related to the books. Some psychic force, or something – like a poltergeist, maybe. You know more about these things than I do. How do you expect the police to deal with it? They're not equipped.'

'The police can't deal with it. But we can.'

'How?'

'We need Sebastian's mirror. It used to belong to Shirley Jackson and he was using it to communicate with her. I'm convinced he inadvertently brought something else through. Something malevolent crossed over into our world when he opened the portal.'

Judy was reminded, for one insane moment, of Ethan, her nephew, a promising young playwright. After the opening night of his latest play, a grand affair in London's West End, he vanished. No word, no note, nothing. He simply disappeared off the face of the earth.

'All right,' she said, 'suppose for one minute I go along with all this. The mirror is at his house. How do we get it? You said his sister wasn't exactly cooperative. She told you the mirror wasn't there.'

'She's lying. It is there.' Freya reached into her bag and produced a set of keys. 'And we get into the house with these. I water Sebastian's plants whenever he's away. We go in through the back door and sneak past her. He'll keep it in the basement – that's where I'd keep it – nice and dark to enhance the etheric forces, the perfect place to summon the dead.'

'We'll be breaking and entering,' Judy said, biting her lip.

'It's not breaking in if you've got keys,' Freya said.

'We'll be trespassing.'

'No we won't. I'm a close friend of Sebastian's. We're there by his invitation. I always water his plants and, at the moment, he can't do it himself. We're just dropping by to give them a drink.'

Judy didn't like the sound of this one bit: Freya's theories of supernatural intervention were mad. She's having some kind of breakdown, Judy thought. She's full of grief and despair and it's affecting her judgement. But equally I can't let her go off on her own. Maybe when it all comes to nothing – when Freya realises you can't talk to dead people through a mirror – she'll see sense.

v

The drawer stuttered open, groaning on its slides. Carefully slotted together in a neat, ordered pile were all the cards Leon had given Tom since they started dating: a Valentine's card, a birthday card and a Christmas card. Next week would have been their one year anniversary. They'd planned a slap-up meal at Brown's. Leon looked out of the window at the neatly mown lawns; the fudge-coloured limestone of the porter's lodge. The gravel path cut a line between the halls and the lodge. He, Tom and Nancy had walked that line just a few nights before on their way to the Shirley Jackson Club. Hadn't Tom said something about seeing a rat? Tears threatened Leon again and he grasped hold of the cards, pushing the drawer shut with his knuckles.

A woman's voice, warm, Irish but with a hard accusatory edge: 'What are you doing in my son's room?' Sally Donnelly was a slight woman, made suddenly older and smaller by the unendurable death of her child.

Although she had never set foot inside Tom's room, she was fiercely protective of everything in it. Every single object would go back home, become a shrine to her son's memory. Leon felt the heat rise in his cheeks. He had every right to be here but he felt like a thief. Illegitimate. Not family. A nasty unspeakable secret.

'I'm a friend of Tom's,' he said, his voice faltering with emotion. 'I just came to get some cards I gave him.' The woman's eyes fell to the bundle in Leon's hand, couldn't fail to see the love hearts, cuddling bears, the words: 'Be My Valentine'. She looked away abruptly as her husband, big, ruddy-faced and broken, came in behind her. 'I'll get out of your way,' Leon said softly. He was nothing now, just an unfortunate detail in the former life of Tom Donnelly. He was a spectre now, nothing but the memory of Tom.

He filled the kettle. He couldn't think about his coursework. His supervisor had given him the week off but he knew the pressure would begin again soon. You couldn't survive Cambridge unless you were a workhorse. He'd thought about going home for a few days but it felt like he'd be abandoning Tom somehow. He started to think of the places they hung out, the things they liked to do: early evening cocktails at the Smokeworks; a curry at the Tiffin Truck; ice creams at Jack's Gelato; a night at Mikey's, the one and only gay club in the city. He sipped his coffee. It was watery and tasteless. He spread the cards on the table and examined them, the doodles and kisses, the affectionate scribblings. He had the strongest sense of Tom's life unlived. Tom had decided to come out to his family; how frightening and powerful that idea had been for him. Now all that was gone; all those possibilities for him, for both of them. Now Tom would never get the chance to be his true self. He had been obliterated – forever now – just no 'self' at all.

Remembering like this had the power to undo him. But at the same time, the feeling of desolation offered up a rare form of sweetness, an estimation of his love. The pain, in proportion to his love lost, was almost like an addiction. He really should do something, try to focus, pull himself together. He thought about Tom and Preet; their deaths so similar to the books at the Shirley Jackson Club. Now was not the time. He needed mundanity, a simple mechanical task. His room was a jumbled mess of overdue library books, dirty cups and half-written essays. With a sigh, he scooped up the cards and left the room.

He met Tom's mother again on the stairs. She didn't return his smile. She looked at him, curiously, as if he were some strange species of sea anemone discovered in the shallow sea surrounding a South Sea island.

'I don't know what hold you had over my son,' Sally Donnelly said. 'How you led him down the path of sin in some hour of weakness when he was too proud or headstrong to confide in his own mother. But I want you to keep away from our family. You are not welcome at my son's funeral and you are not to visit his grave. I will make sure you never find out where my son is laid to rest. As far as I am concerned, you and your kind do not exist.' She descended a few more steps, then turned and looked back at him. 'I pray for your immortal soul.'

chapter nine

"His torso is a man's but his legs and genitals are a wolf's. And he has a wolf's heart."
THE BLOODY CHAMBER | ANGELA CARTER

Gym bunnies, bears, cubs, chubs, otters, pups and spunk monkeys all found their way to Mikey's.

Bindweed brushed stickily against Judy's face. She flicked it away irritably. Her fingers and toes were numb already with cold and her back was aching. All of the nerves in her body seemed at odds: crouching in the undergrowth behind Sebastian's house was all a little bit too 'Scooby-Doo' for words. Common sense was screaming at her not to go along with this. Freya might have keys to Sebastian's house but, to Judy's mind, they were still breaking and entering. Freya was determined and undeflectable. Judy had no choice if she wanted to keep an eye on her. She was startled by the crunch of gravel behind her and Nancy came into view, moving slowly through the gathering dusk so as not to attract attention from anyone inside the house. She peered ahead tentatively then saw Freya beckoning to her.

'All set?' Nancy asked. Freya dangled Sebastian's door keys in front of her.

'She's roped you in too?' Judy said.

'You wait here,' Freya said to Nancy, 'and if you see anything unusual, ring me, my phone's on vibrate.'

'I think you're both very daring,' Nancy said. Judy widened her eyes in mock exasperation.

'When needs must,' said Freya. 'The mirror is the crucial thing.' She tugged at Judy's sleeve. 'Come on.'

Judy looked up at the house: a single lamp burned at a first floor window; the ground floor was in complete darkness. Judy realised she was sweating lightly. Sebastian's house was large, redbrick, Victorian just like a thousand others in Cambridge. But the dark in the downstairs windows hung there unusually, and Judy pictured a black widow waiting to devour its prey. Buck up, she told herself, you're starting to take all of this too seriously.

The tang of moist earth was in the air. The garden was overgrown, savage somehow, in the fitful breeze. Dusk was turning to night; that time of day when everything falls into indeterminacy and shadows take on the shapes of our deepest fears. Freya twisted the key in the lock. It opened with a hollow clunk.

The darkness is cloying, sweet. Judy reaches instinctively for Freya's hand and grasps it tightly. Freya eases the cellar door open and cringes Heep-like as it creaks on its hinges. The steps are narrow and steep and Freya's torch lights only a small arc in front of them, a feeble bulwark against the black. Judy worries about losing her footing. The basement smells strongly of damp and there is another, more unexpected smell, reminiscent of the garden: sodden earth mixed with wet leaves on a forest floor.

The darkness feels thick somehow. Moving through it gives Freya the impression of wading through deep water. Down here, half-buried in the earth, she senses an indescribable force – strong like a radio signal carried on a clear, starry night. The mirror is definitely here.

Judy sees it first, propped up against the wall, a threadbare Egyptian rug spread in front of it, and the whole arrangement surrounded by a circle of black candles. Sebastian's first edition of *We Have Always Lived in the Castle* lies open in the middle. There is something unholy about the mirror. Judy felt it the day she and Freya brought it back from London. The flying gargoyles seem to be looking directly at her, ready to jump free of the frame and sink their teeth into the taut flesh of her throat. Judy is finding it harder and harder to remain a non-believer.

Something ancient and foul and hungry is here in the basement with them. She can smell an acid sweetness as if the darkness were diabetic, sweating and exhaling ketones. She can feel the blood pulling through her veins. It's as if good and evil have been at war in this place, and evil has won the upper hand, nestling itself sweetly in every crack and crevice. Evil begets evil, awakening Judy's most private fears. She is a little girl again, lying awake in the night; afraid of the rabid dog, the killer shark, the Child Catcher. Although Freya is just a few feet away, Judy stands alone before the Devil. She imagines herself trapped in this underground room, something behind her, reaching out with grey, wasted hands to draw her down into hell. Just as it drew her nephew, Ethan.

This is not real, it's silliness, she tells herself. For Christ's sake get a grip. It's just a musty old basement and a tatty old mirror.

'Don't step inside the circle,' Freya hisses urgently. She moves warily around the candles and takes hold of the mirror. Judy guides them by torchlight back to the top of the steps. They pause at the sound of movement from the floors above – something scuttles. 'Let's go,' Freya whispers and Judy has never been so glad to hear those two words in all her life.

ii

Orange painted brickwork and blacked-out windows – a joyless frontage sandwiched between a burger bar and a betting shop: Mikey's – a lugubrious fixture of Hills Road for the past twenty years – had served its purpose well. Mikey's was a beacon, a hub for a particular community in this city of a hundred and forty thousand souls. From Thursday to Monday, Mikey's was home to a pick 'n' mix of gay men looking for incident, connection, sex. Gym bunnies, bears, cubs, chubs, otters, pups and spunk monkeys; all found their way to Mikey's; not because of the friendly atmosphere or the lush decor (God knows the place could do with more than just a lick of paint); not because of the fine wines and sparkling conversation. The men who crammed into the dimly-lit space night after night went there from necessity: Mikey's was the only gay bar in town. And, for many, it was mercifully anonymous. That's what made it so popular with tourists as well as the locals. A night at Mikey's could land you in bed with a handsome guy from anywhere from Argentina to Zimbabwe.

Leon couldn't say how many hours he'd spent pacing the city like a tiger in a cage. He had been wandering aimlessly and everywhere he went, he saw couples and more couples; couples laughing and joking; couples kissing; couples holding hands. Somehow he found himself outside Mikey's and Mikey's drew him in. He had been every week when he first came to Cambridge but less so once he and Tom started dating. Still, they would come, once in a while, to dance and spectate, watching the men of Mikey's searching for something, for someone; and they would huddle close, glad they had no part in that ritual anymore.

Mikey's was the perfect meat market; classic disco beats booming over a mirrored dance floor; clouds of dry ice and the ever-present scent of poppers. Now it was Thursday, not yet midnight. Still early for any self-respecting clubber; the place would be teeming by 1am. Leon glanced towards the bar as he contemplated buying his fourth Jack Daniels and Coke. The musclebound barman, splendid in a tight tee, was serving pints of amber-coloured lager to two suited businessmen – men who looked eager for a quick, forgettable hookup; easily dispensed with before tomorrow's conference speech or team building exercise.

Tonight Leon needed Mikey's like never before. Not for a hookup – he had no desire to meet anyone – and his face told a story of woe dismal enough to deter the most persistent Romeo. No, it was Sally Donnelly who had driven him here. Her words still scratching away inside his head: *You do not exist.*

Right now he wished he didn't. He wanted to disappear, hide away; disappear from people like Sally Donnelly. He needed to be with his own kind; his tribe. He needed to be surrounded by life, and hope. Nightlife and people; the living, not the dead. And most of all he needed to deaden the pain, tear himself free from a world that had lost its song; blot out the unspeakable loss of Tom. For that he had to turn his back on the world beyond Mikey's blackened windows. That world wasn't his, and never could be, because of the way he lived his life.

You do not exist.

Junior school, the last day of term before the Christmas holidays; everyone in a hurry to get the kids home. A friend of his mother's talking about her teenage daughter: still not courting. Rosa had suggested the girl might be lesbian, to which the mother quickly replied: 'No, no, she's not like that. She definitely likes the right sex.' Everyone was in a hurry to get home but not in too much of a hurry to gossip, ridicule, pass judgement. Leon couldn't have been more than eight years old but still the comment cut him, made him feel not right. Back then, he had no idea why.

I pray for your immortal soul.

Every morning, he woke expecting Tom, expecting to see him down in the kitchen, expecting to hear him talking excitedly about a camp old horror film or his latest bookstagram post, expecting to see him smothering his toast with way too much butter. Then the truth would hit like a Boeing striking the South Tower; the death of all his dreams in a blazing fireball. All he wanted was to lie under the bedclothes, imagining Tom still there next to him, talking to him, holding him, loving him.

He shifted his weight; the soles of his trainers stuck to the beer-stained floor. He took a long pull of his Jack Daniels and Coke, draining the last of it, the slice of lime a dirty brown shape in the bottom of the glass. He leaned into the poseur table, unconsciously adopting the stance of the single gay man on his own, staring impassively ahead at nothing in particular. Wait before buying another drink. He'd already gone beyond his limit. He was lightheaded and his blood was pounding in time to Nicki Minaj. The alcohol was having the desired effect at last: Leon Wilson was numb. The numbness was so much better than the other feelings. The only part that wouldn't play along was his bladder. He headed purposefully across the dance floor, knocking into a couple of guys gyrating sensually to the thumping chorus of *Starships*.

There was no door on the men's toilet. The smell of urine and deodoriser blocks laced the air. The place was empty and Leon chose a spot in the farthest corner. He wanted to leave plenty of room between him and any prospective Casanova. He pulled out his penis and began to urinate; the warm honey-coloured jet made a high pitched rattle as it struck the bowl. He fixed his gaze on the rows of once-white tiles, now yellow and cracked, that surrounded the urinals.

Something moves overhead. He looks up at the long rectangular window and sees something moving behind the frosted glass. He can't quite make it out. A balloon? Yes, a red balloon.

Leon zips up his fly. He looks up again but the balloon is gone. He's suddenly very lightheaded, flushed and so very tired. He has to lean against the wall to steady himself; wait for the room to come back into focus. Only problem is: the room isn't coming back into focus. His brain can't connect with his senses properly and everything starts to spin away like he's inside a washing machine. Now, suddenly, a man is lifting him up, walking him outside into the street. He needs the air, the cold hand of the night brings him back to himself.

'Better now?' the man asks, still holding Leon steady. 'You took quite a tumble.'

'I'm fine, I think,' Leon says. 'Thanks for helping.'

'No problem.' The man is impossibly good-looking. His eyes are violet – like Tom's eyes. What's he doing with Tom's eyes? 'Where do you live?' he says. 'Have you far to go?'

'I'm in halls at St Benedict's.'

'I'm not far from there. I'll walk with you, make sure you get home safely.' Leon thinks he hears a dog barking in the distance but no, it's just a car horn. I'm so wasted I'm imagining things, he thinks.

The fast food joints and late night cafés bleed light onto the pavement as they head down Hills Road. The man is not only impossibly good-looking, he's charming too. Soon they're laughing and joking like old friends. Leon is still suffering from the effects of too much alcohol and the man catches him as he stumbles over his own feet.

'I live just in here.' The man nods towards the entrance of a gated complex of townhouses and apartments. 'Let me make you a nice coffee. It'll sober you up. Then I'll walk you back to St Benedict's.' The man's violet eyes – Tom's eyes – smile irresistibly.

'I don't know,' Leon says. 'I should be getting back.' He is suddenly overwhelmed by survivor's guilt; just talking to this man is a betrayal.

'Come on, just for a moment. I promise I don't bite.' The man laughs and his teeth are perfectly straight, perfectly white. Leon follows him dutifully into his house and it occurs to him that he doesn't even know his name.

'By the way, I'm Leon.'

'Carter,' the man smiles. The room has a lovely old brick fireplace with two china spaniels on either side of the mantelpiece. The fire hisses into life like an adder startled in the grass. A colourful rug is spread across the pamment-tiled floor. A Bible lies closed on the table. The fire goes *crack-crack-crack*. Carter disappears into the kitchen.

'Thank you again,' Leon calls, hoping Carter can hear.

'Is there a reward?' Carter replies wolfishly.

'I don't know.'

'How about a kiss?'

Leon feels as if a hunk of ice is being pressed against his stomach. His balls shrivel. This whole thing is a mistake. He moves to go but Carter is at the door, blocking his way. Fear and adrenaline and the sudden racing of his callow blood sharpen Leon's senses. Carter's eyes are red as a bleeding wound.

'Who are you?' Leon's voice trembles and here it comes: the sudden, awful realisation. He knows the answer before he has even finished asking the question.

'Who am I? WHO AM I?'

'Did you kill Tom, and Preet?' And there it is again: the dog barking at the moon, a baleful howl in the leaden chasm of the night.

'Never mind them now,' Carter says. 'There's only we two, my darling. And my brothers in the night. I love the company of wolves.' He tugs up Leon's shirt and thrusts a hairy hand down the front of the boy's jeans. Leon fights the urge to wriggle and squeal like a poor little piggy. Carter throws his head back and howls hungrily. Leon tries to think, tries to remember how this story ends. 'Are you cold, my love?' Leon says, keeping his voice as steady as he can like his life depends on it. (It does.) 'Is that why you are howling so? Come to the fire, dear one, and I'll warm you.' The flames in the fire begin to rise and roar. He takes Carter's paw in his hands and kisses the sharp claws gently.

'My, what big arms you have.'

He leads his red-eyed lover towards the hearth.

'My, what big eyes you have.'

Carter rips off his shirt and his chest is thick with hair, his nipples swollen like ripe berries.

'And what big, big muscles you have.'

Carter strips off his trousers to show how powerful his legs are, how massive his genitals.

'How well-endowed you are, Mr Wolf.'

Leon's heart is racing; his mind is racing too. His head begins to clear. REWRITE! REWRITE! REWRITE!

And so the wolfman squares himself, genitals engorged, and licks his chops. The boy backs slowly away from the horny beast. He takes another step. Then another. And another.

'Don't make me come and get you,' growls the lewd old wolf, 'I long to taste your sweet flesh. You're mine, my beautiful, innocent boy. Mine to eat ALL UP!'

'But you can't fool me,' Leon says, and his voice breaks, brimming with fear. 'This little piggy is nobody's meat. This little piggy knows your game. So I'll huff and I'll puff and I'll blow your house down!'

A gale begins to rise inside the room. It twists and screams and rushes the wolf, flattening his lice-sequinned fur. It fans the fire into a huge, angry blaze. The wolf feels its scorch at his back, and he yelps and he yelps for he is afraid of the fire. The gale is iron-fisted, holding him fast to the spot. He is transfixed. For, even when he leans his full weight into the gale, he cannot advance one inch. Back towards the roaring flames he stumbles. He writhes in panic. He twists, he turns, he fights and he fights but he cannot take another step. Leon turns and runs out of the room. Out of the house.

And he runs and he runs.

Through the lonely night, he runs.

Past the clock that chimes at midnight.

Run run run, little piggy, run, run!

All the way home.

iii

Sebastian pushed himself up on one elbow then swung his legs over the edge of the bed. His feet sank into the carpet furred with dust and dirt. Where was that damned nurse? Couldn't she at least run the hoover over the bloody carpet? He couldn't remember the last time he'd seen her. Last night? Yesterday afternoon? He didn't need her help quite so much now. But she should still buck her ideas up. He couldn't picture her face; just grey hair pulled back into a bun, neck like crepe paper, a constant withering pout. And that old black dress; good God, like an Edwardian housemaid's uniform. He was getting stronger, little by little, but his back still protested. His knee was weak from his fall during the attack. He shuddered. He still relied on

175

a walking stick to get around although he'd managed to cast it aside a couple of times recently. He tested his trembling leg muscles. Brain fog thickened as he stood up, then slowly it began to dissipate. Why still so fragile after all this time? What was holding him down, drawing the life from out of him?

He turned purposefully towards the armchair. He wouldn't use the stick for this little jaunt. He took a couple of tottering steps, pressing tented fingers on the edge of the mattress to steady himself. Then, with a single determined bound, he covered the remaining distance and dropped heavily onto the cushion, wincing at the jarring pain in his back but delighted with his efforts nonetheless. He lifted a newspaper from the stack on the table. God only knows why that bloody nurse left them piled up there. He tried to remember her name. Mangen? Morgen? Was that her first name or her surname? Where had he heard the name before? Crepey, pouty Nurse Whatever-her-name-was knew full well he preferred to read the papers in bed. But still she left them over by the chair.

He needed to let that go – for his own sake. Freya would be the first to remind him that the body is the servant of the mind. She used to say holding onto anger is like holding a hot coal you want to throw at someone else but you just end up burning yourself. Or words to that effect. The papers weren't much use to him at the moment; he'd been so dosed up, he was barely able to concentrate. Morgen was doing her best but there was something about her he couldn't quite put his finger on. Was it just that she was so mannish? And he was an old fashioned sort? She had an essentially masculine gruffness about her. And that name – where had he heard it before?

He reached into the pocket of his dressing gown and pulled out his spectacles. He tipped the paper to the light and read the headline. A boy, a student from St Benedict's, had been gnawed to death by rats. The boy was Tom Donnelly; lovely little Tom from the book group. Sebastian's lips moved silently, as if in prayer. He remembered Freya's visit. Something had happened but she wouldn't tell him what. He tried to cast his mind back into the fog.

Someone had a strange encounter… but not with the clown…

Sebastian leafed quickly through the rest of the newspapers in the pile. And there it was: the horrific murder of a young woman, another student from St Benedict's, Preet Chanda, murdered by a knife to the throat and a child was somehow involved. Sebastian put the paper down, breathing slowly and deeply, trying to keep calm. He pressed his knuckles to his forehead in an attempt to compel his addled brain to work. *Don't Look Now.* He'd read it years ago. Who could forget the closing lines, the figure in the pixie-hood? He was certain now. These things had happened because of him. He hadn't left his room since he came home from hospital but he had to get down to his library now; he had to dig out the Daphne du Maurier, *The Rats*, and the definitive treatise on the supernatural: Ruth Christie's *European Demonology and Folklore*. His arms shook with the effort of getting up out of the chair. He leaned heavily on his stick. He reached unsteadily for the doorknob and the door opened startlingly, the spindly frame of Nurse Morgen like a preying mantis in the doorway. There was something utterly soulless about her. She scuttled towards him – 'scuttle' was the only word to describe it – causing him to stumble. Her bone-white face creased into a mirthless grin.

'And where do you think you're going, kiddo?'

Kiddo? Kiddo? Why did she always bloody call him kiddo? Then it came to him: Morgen was a character in *The Bird's Nest* by Shirley Jackson.

With one lightning movement, Nurse Morgen grabbed him by the collar.

And punched him in the face.

iv

Freya was pacing up and down the kitchen. Her voice grew louder with her frustration. 'For pity's sake, Judy, Leon was attacked by whatever attacked Preet, and attacked Tom, and Sebastian!' She counted out the names on her fingers for emphasis.

Judy mustered all the middle-aged sangfroid she could: 'All I'm saying is, we should at least try and look for a more rational explanation. Maybe Leon was suffering from alcohol poisoning when it happened. He'd just lost Tom. He was dead drunk. Maybe his overwrought imagination conjured up a wolf when in truth he was attacked by something far more prosaic – another human being, a man with the same predatory intentions as so many others, nothing more than that.'

'Too many people have been killed just to dismiss this out of hand.'

'That's not fair.'

'All right. I'm sorry. But just look at our reading list: *It*.

Don't Look Now.

The Rats.

The Company of Wolves.

And now Leon is attacked by a man turned wolf in front of his eyes.'

'His very drunk eyes. I know full well all the terrible things that have happened, Freya.'

'We have to DO something. You or I might be next!'

'What did Inspector Sorensen say?'

'Not much. Apart from the fact that the house where Leon encountered the wolfman —'

'Believes he encountered a wolfman.'

'That house had been empty for months.'

'Isn't it entirely possible that some sadist, into young men, staked out that house first then lured Leon back there to attack him? Or maybe the attacker was a squatter?'

Freya folded her arms and stared up at the ceiling as if asking for help from on high. 'I'm telling you Judy, Leon was attacked by a werewolf or something able to take on the form of a wolf.' She snatched up her copy of *The Bloody Chamber* and began flipping through the pages. '*Two china spaniels with liver-coloured blotches on their coats and black noses sit on either side of the fireplace.* That's from *The Company of Wolves*. Leon said there were two china spaniels on either side of the fireplace. He said the fireplace was old like something you'd find in a country cottage not a developer's hutch in the centre of Cambridge.'

'I don't think we can infer Beelzebub is after us because Leon saw a couple of china dogs. What we need to know is what Leon's assailant did to make him imagine he saw these things?'

Freya stood with her hands on her hips, 'Leon and Nancy believe me even if you don't.'

There was a lengthy silence.

Judy sighed and massaged her forehead with long slender fingers. 'You know how incredibly hard this is for me. To my mind, a person, or a group of people, have to be behind all this. Someone with a vendetta against you, or Persephone's, or maybe they're just a lunatic.' She paused, took a deep breath, and let it out slowly. 'But let's just say, for one insane moment, I go along with this theory of yours. What on earth are we supposed to do about it? The police are never going to believe you.'

'The police won't be able to do anything. We need an expert.'

'What kind of expert?'

'Shirley Jackson.'

'You're back onto that?'

'Hear me out,' Freya said. 'Some people believe it's possible to communicate with the spirit world using an object connected with the deceased. Think of the physical object as a bridge between worlds. We use the mirror as a *psychomanteum*.' Judy's blank expression said it all. 'It's a term used in parapsychology and Spiritualism,' Freya said. 'We place the mirror in a darkened room, angled so as to reflect nothing but darkness. It then becomes a means of communication. Sebastian used the mirror for inspiration and unwittingly opened a portal through which something evil came.'

Judy's instinct was to reject the idea out of hand. She fought that instinct hard. 'I'm listening,' she said.

'We summon Shirley Jackson and ask for her help.'

'Then what?'

'Then we fight whatever this thing is, and destroy it.'

Judy threw up her hands. 'You and I, and a couple of frightened kids are going out into the night like *Buffy the Vampire Slayer*?'

'So we can't save the world,' Freya was nodding her head, 'because we're just a pair of old dykes?'

Now it was Judy's turn to fold her arms. 'I wouldn't put it quite like that.' She hated quarrelling at the best of times and she specially hated quarrelling with Freya. She wished everything could go back to the way it used to be; afternoon walks hand-in-hand along the Cam; cosy little lunches and dinners at Brown's; a pot of tea and a Chelsea bun at Fitzbillies. She wished Preet and Tom were alive, and Leon and Sebastian unharmed. She felt Freya's arm around her shoulders.

'I know all this seems strange,' Freya said. 'And I know I'm a nutty old witch who loves smudging and tarot cards and dancing naked in the woodlands at sunset. But we've got to do something before someone else gets hurt. Or killed. Humour me. Just this once. If it all comes to nothing then we'll do it your way. Or Inspector Sorensen's. But let's at least *try*.'

Judy looked at her sombrely, then, after a moment, a smile flickered across her face. 'All right. Just this once, you old witch.'

chapter ten

"We are all measured, good or evil, by the wrong we do to others; I had made a monster and turned it loose upon the world."
THE BIRD'S NEST | SHIRLEY JACKSON

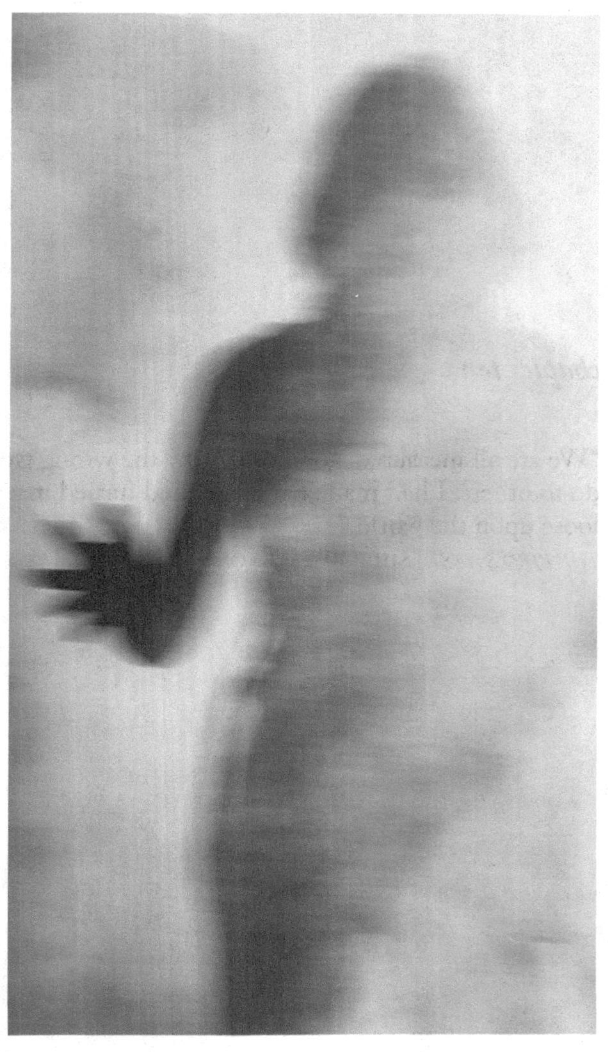

As she turned towards them, her features detached themselves from the swirling fumata bianca.

Freya moved purposefully around her sitting room, lighting candles like a priest preparing for Mass. She'd been high priestess of her coven for almost fifteen years. Every ritual – Yule, Ostara, Beltane, Samhain, handfastings, initiations – she'd overseen them all. Now she found herself in uncharted waters, and it thrilled and frightened her. Sebastian's mirror was propped on the mantelpiece; Judy, Leon and Nancy stood solemnly in front of it. Freya lit the last candle and turned the lights down low. Now she began to move in a wide circle, holding a wooden athame in her right hand as if she were drawing an invisible line through the air. When she completed the circle, she put the wand away and returned to the others. This was her domain, her country. She intended to show them the seasoned crone, the wise and practised witch despite any uncertainties she felt lurking just beneath the surface. To Judy, she seemed supremely confident; a Zen-like calm issued from her and it lent her a lovely, numinous beauty.

'The circle I've drawn around us delineates a safe and sacred space,' Freya said gravely. 'Nothing can harm us as long as we remain inside. No one must leave the circle until the ritual is complete.'

Freya threw her arms open, her head back and began to call the quarters: 'Spirits of the earth, I call on you to join us in this circle. Hail and welcome. Elements of the air, I call on you to join us in this circle. Hail and welcome. Spirits of the fire, elements of water, I call on you to join us in this circle. Hail and welcome.' With each pronouncement, she faced in a new direction until she had turned one full circle. She instructed Judy, Leon and Nancy to form a ring by holding hands. 'I want you to close your eyes and picture Shirley Jackson in your minds. Say her name out loud with me.'

> 'Shirley Hardie Jackson,
> Shirley Hardie Jackson,
> Shirley Hardie Jackson.'

Judy was having a hard time giving credence to any of this. She was acutely aware of herself standing in Freya's sitting room, in front of an old mirror, calling out a dead author's name. She felt ridiculous. She did as she was asked because it was important to Freya.

When this was over they could all sit down, perhaps, and really work out what to do. Rationally. Objectively. With the police leading the investigation. And hopefully Freya wouldn't have lost too much face. New Age people were always explaining away the failure of a god, icon or avatar to appear – the conditions weren't right; it was too cold, too hot; the wrong incantation; the wrong location; the participants' faith just wasn't strong enough. As far as Judy could tell, nothing was happening; no rapid change in temperature, no rising winds, no sound of distant bells.

She opened her eyes a fraction and looked at the others. Leon, Nancy and Freya stood with their eyes tightly shut, bodies leaning back slightly, pulling a little against each other's hands, holding each other in perfect tension. Judy felt that tension too. Then she saw white smoke, like the *fumata bianca* that announces a new Pope, swirling in the mirror. She looked around for the source of the smoke. Had one of the candles set something alight, a runner or a curtain? Nothing. No voracious flames licking up towards the ceiling. She looked back to the mirror. 'Oh, my God,' she whispered. The others jumped at the unexpected sound, breaking the connection.

'Jeepers!' Nancy said.

Leon caught his breath.

Freya looked relieved; and suddenly younger.

In the mirror, the smoke was growing whiter and thicker, overwhelming the reflection of the four members of the Shirley Jackson Club. Then, in the laundry-white mass, the form of a woman appeared, her back turned. The air above the surface of the mirror scintillated in the dark, charged suddenly with an odd form of static, like an electrical storm in miniature. Judy felt the sudden humidity against her skin. She resisted the urge to rub her eyes. The little storm started to break with a shower of sparks and a rumbling of thinnish thunder. Leon and Nancy were dumbstruck. The woman in the mirror wore a pale grey cardigan and her auburn hair fell untidily over rounded shoulders. As she turned towards them, her features detached themselves from the swirling *fumata bianca*: face and neck, plump; nose supporting cat-eye glasses. Behind the flashing lenses; her eyes a vivid, watery green.

'Shirley Jackson?' Freya asked tentatively. The tilt of the head, the raised eyebrows, the crease at the corner of the mouth, all expressed the author's lack of amusement.

'Why have you brought me here?' she asked. Her American accent was soft, her voice unhurried and assured but her tone was barbed. 'I'm busy!'

'I need to know if you are really Shirley Jackson.'

'I am,' Jackson smiled sardonically, 'Shirley Jackson, writer, housewife and witch. Not always in that order.'

'How do we know you're not a deception, a shapeshifter?'

'You're just going to have to take my word for it, aren't you?'

'When were you born?' Freya persisted.

'December fourteenth, nineteen sixteen, San Francisco.'

'When did you die?'

'August eighth, sixty-five. I just went upstairs one afternoon and never came down again. Alive, that is.' Jackson paused; that tilt of the head again. 'Satisfied?'

'Yes,' Freya said obediently. 'We've called you because we need your help. Our friend Sebastian – '

'Oh Sebastian!' Jackson nodded her head. 'You must be

in England. Am I right? Where they make the Morris Minors. I love Morris Minors, oddest little things on four wheels. I owned a few.' She smiled approvingly and the embers of a deeply happy memory lit up her features. 'Oh yes, Sebastian Sizemore, what a delightful man. Horror writers are generally the most gentle of people. Did you know that? I remember saying to Sebastian how everybody deserves a good scare. Most people, lying there in their beds at night, will believe in all sorts of dark and frightening things. My husband, Stanley, liked to pride himself on how practical he was. He used to scold me for practising witchcraft, for believing in ghosts. Then he couldn't read *Hill House* because it scared the bejesus out of him! Can you believe that?' She paused at the thought and this time her smile was broad, her eyes triumphant. 'So how's Sebastian's book going? I told him he needed to get it serialised in a magazine. Reel them all in, get everyone whipped up into a vituperative frenzy.' She chuckled to herself. 'He said he'd inscribe the book 'To S with love from S' just like Stanley and I used to do.'

'Sebastian's finished the book,' Freya said.

'Any good?'

'Not bad.'

'Only not bad? Oh dear.' Jackson lowered her chin and cast a rueful gaze downwards like a gambler with a godawful hand. 'Maybe I wasn't any use to him after all. Maybe I'm past it. Maybe he should have flipped through the Tarot for inspiration – I swear by the Tarot of Marseilles. But you can always use the Waite Smith if you're in a bind.' She reached down and began fumbling for something; next the sound of match against matchbox and her face lit up with a buttery glimmer. Her hand came into view holding a cigarette. She took the long, slow drag of an experienced smoker, gratification spreading, like religious feeling on the face of a saint, across her features.

'You know,' she said as she blew a stream of smoke from the corner of her mouth, 'there's nothing more satisfying than being a writer. It can be backbreaking work – no doubt about that – but if you can get into the rhythm of a piece, get right down there in the belly of the beast, the rewards are spectacular.'

Her lips closed around her Pall Mall more philosophically this time. 'Every writer needs her own library, lovingly built up over the years. Your very lifeblood runs through those shelves. God, I miss my library. I had hundreds of books on witchcraft. Hundreds! Frazer's *The Golden Bough* was by far and away the best. I first discovered it at Rochester, used it to write a term paper on witchcraft. It is one helluva book. It scandalised everyone when it came out. There's nothing like a good scandal for those book sales, is there?' She chuckled again, a razor-cut-paper kind of a chuckle.

'*The Golden Bough*,' Freya said, 'has undoubtedly influenced many of the 20th Century's most creative writers.'

'You have my attention!'

'When Sebastian called you through the *psychomanteum*, something else came through as well, something horribly malevolent now causing the most appalling harm in our world.'

'Didn't Sebastian use protections? Potions? Protective symbols?

'He didn't.'

'For God's sake! Goddam amateurs!' Jackson lit up with

anger. 'It doesn't take much. A simple charm on a window sill will keep most demons at bay. But then, who really needs to worry about demons? The greatest evil is right up in here,' she tapped her forefinger three times at her temple, 'in the human soul. That's where the trouble starts.' She cast her gaze upwards as if retrieving something from the distant recesses of memory. 'Jay Williams, a friend of Stanley's, summoned up the Devil once. Right there in the room with us. I was too frightened to look. Afterwards, he gave me a little book of black magic, told me I could use it to conjure the Devil, ask him for anything... But you'd have to be a damned fool. There's always a price to pay. I wrapped the book in silk and hid it away.'

'Is there anything you can do to help us with the demon in our midst? It's already killed two members of our little group. And I know it's going to kill again.'

Jackson just stared at her. Then she pressed her face against the mirror, moving slowly and tenderly, as if she were making love to the glass. She moved her face ritualistically up and down, her cheeks pressing white against the hard glass surface, wrinkling the skin under her eyes. Finally, she straightened up. 'From what I can gather, something not altogether savoury did come through,' she said, 'and it's feeding its fat face on your imaginations. It's been using them collectively to manifest 'situations' shall we say? That's all I can tell you.' She paused, frowning for a moment. 'You said you were a little group. What kind of group?'

Freya cleared her throat. 'We're all members of a reading group and we call ourselves the Shirley Jackson Club.'

Jackson's grin was broad and deep.

'We're fans,' Nancy said.

'Have you got cats?' Jackson asked. 'You should all get cats. Every single one of you. Everybody should have at least one black cat. And I mean real black – deep, deep coal black.' She tipped her head inquisitively, offering a fond smile like an encouraging parent. 'Is it just me you read? I'm flattered but you could cast your net wider. There's some great writing out there: Ralph Ellison is such a gifted author. He often used to come visit us, Stanley and me.'

'We do read other authors,' Freya said, 'but always horror writers.'

Jackson looked a little stunned, shaking her head, almost imperceptibly, from side to side. 'Then you really are in a fix. This bad ol' demon lives inside books. If you've been feeding him horror stories... My oh my, very bad idea.'

Now the *fumata bianca* returned, thickening and swirling around Shirley Jackson, whitening the glass. Gradually it darkened, turning black as soot like the *fumata nera* rising high above the Sistine Chapel when the cardinals have failed to select a new Pope. Shirley Jackson was almost gone.

'What do you mean, the demon lives inside books?' Freya asked.

Jackson opened her mouth to speak: 'It's very, very ancient...' But her words were lost in the fumata's dark particles.

Shirley Jackson was gone.

The glass was silver once again and showed Freya, Judy, Nancy and Leon nothing but themselves.

'Get her back!' Nancy gasped.

'We can't,' Freya said. 'The *psychomanteum* has closed and we mustn't open it again, at least for a while. Reopening it too soon would create instability between our two worlds. I suspect that's how the problem came about in the first place.'

'So what do we do now?' Leon asked.

'We have to find the identity of our unwelcome visitor. Then work out how to destroy it.'

'She said the demon lives inside books,' Judy said. 'Do you know what she meant?'

'At this point,' Freya frowned, 'I really haven't a clue.'

ii

Sebastian was floating in black oil, drifting on a wide, slow current towards aqueous light. Now he was conscious of lying on the floor and he could see all the way under his bed: the carpet was woolly with dust. The carpet's pile tickled his cheek maddeningly. He hauled himself back onto the bed, limbs protesting at the effort. There was a dull throbbing along one side of his face; he rubbed his aching jaw. Then it came back to him: nurse Morgen had hit him. He looked around. The room was undisturbed. He listened for a few moments; there was no sound to indicate she was still in the house. He waited until he felt less shaky then retrieved his walking stick from the floor.

The landing was choked with shadow like a thick weight shifting around him; or an intelligence even, conscious enough and clever enough to be watching him, biding its time. The floorboards creaked, announcing his location as he looked over the banisters into the dark hallway below. Otherwise the silence in the house was absolute; as cold and barren as the moon. Carefully, he made his way down the stairs, planting his forearm against the wall to steady himself. He was struck by the smell of wet leaves and muddy earth; the smell of the outside oozing in, taking up occupation inside the house.

Usually he found comfort in the tick-tock of the grandfather clock but now it spoke of time running away, isolation, vulnerability. Each 'tick' fuddled his brain a little. *Tick*. It was, he imagined, like the 'drip, drip, drip' of Chinese water torture. *Tick*. Sebastian shook his head. *Tick*. He focused all of his attention on the bookshelves, breathing in the literary spices of old ink and yellowed paper, the smell of time itself. *Tick*. Light splashed in through the windows from the street-lamp outside. *Tick*. He picked up the pace as his eyes accustomed themselves to the semi-gloom. *Tick*. He flicked through his first edition of *Not After Midnight*, revisiting the appalling climax of *Don't Look Now*.

He took off his glasses as if avoiding the horror of what had happened to Preet, and to Tom. The thick of night was closing in around him. Two young lives snuffed out in a matter of seconds. But the point of power is always now, he reasoned, and he had the power to fight this evil, to stop any more killing. He ran his finger along the shelves and there it was: *European Demonology and Folklore* by Ruth Christie. Great writer, and a great friend although he hadn't seen her in a long while. He remembered a panel discussion they'd both been part of on Radio 4 back in the eighties; something about the power of fiction to influence reality; the dangers of horror stories being reenacted by the young and impressionable. It was around the time of the brouhaha about the Video Recordings Act and the banning of 'video-nasties'. He and Ruth had argued against the idea that certain films made violence exciting and seductive; that images of violence could lead to actual crimes. Ruth must be in her late nineties now, he thought, and still unstoppable. He'd read somewhere that she had a new book coming out soon – what an old firecracker she was! He took *European Demonology and Folklore* down from the shelf and sat at his desk. He turned on the reading lamp and flipped through the index. It didn't take him long to find what he was looking for. Here was the culprit: Leshi. He was sure of it. He turned to the relevant page:

Leshi, also Leshy: a demon-like entity of the forest found in Slavic folklore. A mischievous pagan demon, Leshi is able to change shape at will, assuming a rich variety of forms including wild animals like bears, wolves and crows. Leshi is also able to reproduce entire landscapes such as woodlands or forests. Leshi has been known to impersonate domesticated animals and also human beings, either living, dead or fictional. Manifestations of Leshi are often induced by fear felt by an individual or a group of individuals. According to ancient lore, Leshi lives in ancient trees, in hollows and stumps, as well as in fallen logs. Leshi is a consummate mimic and, in its various guises, the demon seeks to terrify, confuse and even kill its victims. It feeds on fear and seeks its revenge on any who harm or damage the woodlands under its protection. The demon is often considered to be a hostile and malevolent supernatural entity and is angered by the felling of trees.

Leshi is only afraid of the thing that is most destructive to the forest – fire. The demon is fascinated by human activity and particularly the stories that people tell each other and will often listen, from a safe distance in the shadows, to supernatural tales told around the campfire. Such stories provide Leshi with the imaginative fuel for its mischievous and often destructive manifestations. Leshi will harvest these stories and, in some instances, seek out concrete objects related to them to help it perfect its shapeshifting. Leshi is the magpie of the forest, purloining anything that catches its attention, as well as abducting the innocent and vulnerable who lose their way in the woods at sunset. Leshi can be summoned by calling out the words: 'Leshi, I summon you. Reveal yourself to me, not as a wolf, nor as a raven, nor as a towering tree, but as I command it.'

Sebastian closed the book and returned his reading glasses to his pocket.

He went into the hall to telephone Freya – and prayed he wasn't too late.

'Sebastian! Are you all right?'

'Apart from being assaulted in my own home, I'm fine.'

'Did someone break in? Have you called the police?'

'It's not the sort of thing you call the police about.'

'Is your sister there with you? Was she hurt as well?'

'Freya, my dear, I don't have a sister.'

There was a pause before Freya spoke again. 'Sebastian, you need to leave the house now. The woman I took to be your sister is a demon.'

'I'm well aware of that. It also posed as my nurse and attacked me. The demon is called Leshi. It's a forest demon and it's feeding on the fear provoked in us by the books we love to read. It has been killing, fuelled by the thrill of our terror and our dismay.'

'Bloody hell!' Freya muttered. 'How did I not see it? Books come from paper, paper comes from trees.'

'It won't be long before Leshi is powerful enough to go

beyond our little book group and rain down terror on the rest of the world.'

'We may have reached that point already.'

'It's my fault. I allowed it through. The youngsters died because of me.'

A lump rose in Freya's throat. 'Don't think about that now. We have to find a way to destroy it or send it back across the divide. There'll be plenty of time for regret later.'

iii

'How do we kill it?' Nancy asked, picking at her nails absently, producing a little volley of nervous clicks.

'Sebastian and I have come up with a plan,' Freya said, looking at her three companions steadily. 'Leshi is a demon of the forest, so it's afraid of fire. I think that was proven conclusively by Leon's encounter with it. There's an old derelict mansion on the outskirts of Cambridge: Pendleton Manor. We lure Leshi there, and then we burn the whole thing to the ground. I keep a couple of cans of petrol in the boot of my VW in case of emergencies.'

'Arson?' from Judy.

'I think we're beyond questions of legality now,' Freya replied.

'How do we lure it, exactly?' Leon asked.

'We need copies of every book we've read at the group. And they must be our own copies, the books we've handled, bonded with. Some from me, some from each of you.' She looked from Judy to Leon to Nancy.

'Leon and I will go and get our books from halls,' said Nancy, 'and we'll meet you at the manor.'

'Leshi will also be attracted by objects or symbols

associated with the stories,' said Freya. 'We need something connected with one or more of the books to help us reel Leshi in.'

'What about Lemarchand's box from *The Hellbound Heart*?' Leon said.

'You're a bloody genius!' Freya said. She answered Judy's puzzled expression: '*The Hellbound Heart* was the very first book we read. Lemarchand's box resembles a black, lacquered Chinese puzzle. There's a replica of it at the shop, a prop. Whoever solves the puzzle summons the Cenobites, demonic creatures from an alternate dimension who were themselves once human. They metamorphosed into Cenobites because of their relentless pursuit of physical experience, both ecstatic and agonising.'

Judy winced. 'Sounds awful.'

'It's brilliant.' Freya winked. 'If we survive tonight, I'll read it to you.' She turned back to Leon. 'Judy and I will get the box from the shop. You two bring copies of everything on the reading list from *The Hellbound Heart* to *Frankenstein*. We'll bring the rest. And we'll meet at Pendleton in one hour.'

Leon was already standing.

The front door slammed behind the two students. Judy grabbed her coat. Freya cast around for her car keys. Judy touched her arm. 'I'm sorry I doubted you,' she said quietly. The distance between the two women closed suddenly. Judy found herself standing on the shore of a new land a very long way from bereavement and loneliness; a land, nevertheless, that frightened her a little because of the risks involved. Freya smiled and kissed her tenderly on the cheek.

'Come on,' she said, 'these two old dykes have got to save the world, remember?'

chapter eleven

"Outside they howled and pummeled the door,
shouting his name in a paroxysm of demented fury."
I AM LEGEND | RICHARD MATHESON

*Limbs flailing, voices appalling, they beat the doors
with their fists, break open the barred way.*

i

A black lacquered cube, seven centimetres square, intricate yellow patterns adorning every surface. Judy wasn't familiar with the symbology but she could see Lemarchand's Box was beautiful and perhaps that was the point; just beneath the beautiful surface lies a profound, corrupting evil. Freya's description of *The Hellbound Heart* had put Judy on edge. She prayed Leshi would overlook that particular story; she had no desire to meet the Cenobites. Freya disappeared into her office to find the key to the display cabinet. Judy looked at the tables stacked with books on druidism, cosmology, demonology, the history of ritual sacrifice. The volumes in Persephone's described the best and worst of human imaginings.

There was something eerie about a bookshop late at night, Freya admitted. Whenever she was working late, passersby would see the dim interior light, someone or something moving about, and think the shop was haunted. No, a bookshop should be full of bright morning sunlight, dotted about with people perusing the shelves, looking for fascinating companions for the train or the bus or the airport lounge. Instead there was a deadness in the air at night, an empty feeling that made Judy's scalp tingle. She shivered involuntarily. They had to defeat the creature, Leshi, or it would draw power from every wicked book ever written: *The Malleus Maleficarum, The Prince, The Lesser Key of Solomon, Mein Kampf.* It would be open season on the written word. And the human race. Leshi could cause whole continents to rise up against one another, faith against faith, nation against nation. And it would all be so easy. God, it could even start World War Three.

Freya returned, handing Judy copies of *The Woods Are Dark, The Bloody Chamber* and *The Rats.*

She lifted Lemarchand's box out of the display case, holding it up admiringly. 'Hopefully we have enough to tempt the demon into the open,' she said. 'All we need now are the last couple of books from your place.'

Freya's rusty VW Beetle chugged determinedly towards the city centre. Its rattling engine protested against the damp night. The city was deserted. The people of Cambridge were snug and safe behind locked doors, unaware of what was hiding in their mist-shrouded city. Something artful and hungry was readying itself, looking to sate its unnatural appetite on the unspoken contents of their minds, looking for the things they did not dare to look at themselves when they shuddered awake in the middle of the night.

The theatre of battle was set now for the surviving members of the Shirley Jackson Club.

The little car weaved its way in the direction of Eden Street. Everyday sights came into vivid relief, comfortingly familiar things Judy so easily took for granted: the slender, huddled punts at Magdalene Bridge; the smart expanse of Jesus Green; the honey-orange sign of The Free Press. Judy wondered if this were the last time she would see any of these beloved things.

The hallway of 94 Eden Street was silent. This house had once enclosed a world of cosy routines, shared stories and intimate laughter. Now the atmosphere was out of kilter in an indefinable and undermining way.

'The books are on a shelf in my bedroom,' Judy said quietly. 'Shan't be a tick.' Freya nodded and waited in the living room, hands deep in the pockets of her dungarees. She looked absentmindedly at the painting above the wood burner: a yacht in full sail under a stormy sky, shadow darkening its sails, greying its sleek white hull.

The stairs creaked cunningly under Judy's footfall. She stopped halfway. Had something moved upstairs?

Silence reasserted itself.

Get a grip, you old fool, she thought.

Her bedroom door moaned lightly on its hinges. She fetched *I Am Legend* and *Not After Midnight*, and returned to the landing. Now there definitely was a sound, a movement, like someone turning over in their sleep. The door to the guest room was ajar and the dullest light spilled gloomily onto the landing. Judy was afraid but also maddeningly, uncharacteristically curious. Too much time with Freya, she thought.

Her imagination conjured indistinct terrors: peculiar fantasies, fragments from her past. Now she was a little girl and her parents had gone out to a masonic ladies night. They had left her older brother, Peter, in charge of the house, in charge of her. As she got ready for bed, she heard Peter calling her name: 'Judy!' She followed the sound to his room but he was nowhere to be seen. She stood stock still, listening for him to call again but the house was silent. Then, as she turned to go, he leapt out of the wardrobe, growling like a mad dog. She screamed and he roared with laughter, a chauvinist's sadistic laughter at her expense – silly little frightened girl.

And here she was, frightened again. Common sense cried out, go no further, but the urge was undefeatable. She pressed the tips of her fingers against the door and pushed it open.

Greta was lying on the bed. She was dressed in a simple white funeral gown just as she had been when Judy saw her for the very last time. Her hair was in its usual bob-cut, but brushed away from her face. In death, like so many before her, her face displayed an ultimate beauty, delivered absolutely from the woes of living. There was the faintest trace of conceit on her face, suggesting an undeclared knowledge of worlds that lay, for now, beyond Judy's grasp. One arm rested gently across her waist, the other was lying at her side. Greta was an artfully presented corpse. Judy was drawn to her in spite of herself. She harboured the insane hope of the still grieving: that Greta had come back to her for reasons godly rather than otherwise. They could simply pick up where they'd left off, take up their homely little life again, like picking up your knitting. In this excruciating moment, Judy realised how much she longed for the return of old certainties.

She wanted Greta to look up at her and tell her all this was fiction. There was no Shirley Jackson Club, no Persephone's. There had been no gruesome killings. Tom Donnelly and Preet Chanda were alive and well in their rooms, absorbed in their studies, a mug of tea and a packet of biscuits in easy reach. Judy longed for that mundane, ordinary world. The idea of wickedness, of quotidian evil, was foolishness, just a bad dream. Deep inside, she knew hoping like this was its own kind of madness, a pathological, naive optimism. In spite of feeling so afraid, Judy smiled at her own stupidity. And it was as if her smile made sound enough to wake the dead. Greta opened her eyes. They were callous not kind eyes, inky-black, lightless. Greta looked at Judy with a perverse smile. Her teeth were white and sharp.

Judy realised what a mistake it had been to come into this room: the thing lying there was not her wife.

'Look at me,' Greta says. The voice is clear and crisp; it sounds like Greta except underneath is something darker, not a human voice at all. Judy has no choice but to look into Greta's eyes. They draw her in, sweetly, hypnotically; she can see the image of herself in the glossy domes of the corneas as she leans over the bed. Now Judy is falling into those eyes, into a warm place, a thick, dark suffocating place. Greta is rising from the mattress, her breath close and chill when it should be warm on Judy's face. Her lips, closer and closer to Judy's lips, moving now to the unprotected flesh of Judy's throat.

'Out!' Judy hears Freya's voice from behind her. 'Get out! I command it. You are not welcome here. Out I say! Leave this body, befouling spirit!' Freya advances towards them in the airless room, become great witch or benign goddess, something as old, or older, than Leshi; divine lesbian. 'You are not welcome in this house!'

Greta hisses involuntarily like a startled cat. Freya is holding a Celtic cross in front of her, advancing towards the thing-that-would-be-Greta like a pontiff of the great and ancient religion of the Celts or an Imperial Archdruid capable of flying the stones of Stonehenge into position by power of mind alone.

The thing-in-the-shape-of-Greta flinches, still holding Judy's gaze: 'I'll see you sleep like the dead, my love.' It leaps through the window in a screaming shower of glass. Freya looks down to the paving stones below but the thing is already gone. She turns to find Judy crouching on the floor, her hand clamped tightly over her mouth, her shoulders shuddering, tears rolling down her stricken face. Freya puts her hands on Judy's shoulders and gently pulls her up, hugging her trembling body.

'It's over now,' she said. 'It can't hurt you now.'

'But I thought it was...'

'It wasn't. It was another manifestation of Leshi.'

'Why would it pretend to be...?' Judy couldn't bring herself to say her dead wife's name.

'I don't know,' Freya told her. 'Perhaps now it can reach beyond the books we've read to our most painful memories. Perhaps it's like a ventriloquist, throwing its voice, beguiling us, harvesting our stories, mixing memory and desire to deceive and destroy us!' Freya spoke with such force Judy stopped crying and looked up at her. Freya said, 'A vampire in the bedroom is from *Salem's Lot*. 'I'll see you sleep like the dead' is from King's text. We're really in trouble now.'

'Why?'

'Because we haven't read *Salem's Lot* at the club. *I've* read it – quite a few years back now. Leshi has become powerful enough to mix your memories and mine. We must hurry before it becomes impossibly adept, impossibly powerful to defeat.'

Judy stood up. She thought of her lovely Greta and how Leshi had stolen and manipulated her image, bastardised her into something deceptive and vile. Leshi had played on Judy's simple desire to have her wife back. Now she knew she had no further to fall. 'Let's get to Pendleton Manor,' Judy said, 'and kill this thing.'

ii

Leon's mind was full of Freya's Leshi: a demon of the forest that plays tricks on the unwary; a monstrous apparition that feeds on fear and anxiety. So Leshi was the thing that had taken Tom away from him. Tom with his pale, freckled skin; eyes smiling behind cute little wire-framed Windsor glasses; Tom who he had been planning a whole life with. Tom dead now, his family never knowing who he really was. So much unseen, unexpressed, unrealised. All the potential of a man. Leshi had reduced the man he loved to tissue and bone.

Know thine enemy.

Leon stared ahead, fists clenched, looking but not seeing. He wanted to be there at the kill. No – he wanted to make the kill.

Know thine enemy.

Nancy's thoughts were also somewhere beyond the interior of the speeding taxi. Her first month at Cambridge. Even though her parents lived in Chesterton, she'd never wanted to spend her student years at home. She wanted independence; escape from their stifling conservatism and small-time entrepreneurialism. 'English Literature – why on earth? Where's the value? You can't earn good money with a degree like that!' Escape from her annoying, prank-playing younger brothers: 'Put your hand in there. It's nothing nasty. Honest.' Living in college meant her own space, the beginning of her great escape. Horror night in Tom's room; Tom and Leon lounging on the bed; she and Preet cross-legged on cushions on the floor; Tom's laptop perched on a chair; the lights down low. Linda Hayden, vengeful and determined, about to blast Karl Howman with both barrels in the middle of an Essex wheat field. Cute and sexy Karl Howman with the nicest eyes. Why did he have to die? Why did Tom have to die? Why did Preet have to die? Horror night was Tom's idea, an antidote to the Sunday evening blues before another week of study and supervision. He had everything from *The Curse of Frankenstein* to *Dog Soldiers*. Leon always steered him towards a camp classic from the sixties or seventies: *Doctor Blood's Coffin, Night of the Eagle, Brides of Dracula*. The first film their little group watched was *The Beast Must Die*, a 1974 production by Amicus, the poor cousin of mighty Hammer studios. Guests at a country house must uncover the werewolf among them. Tom could recall every bit of trivia about the film: *The Beast Must Die* had a 'werewolf break' near the end of the film – the audience was given thirty seconds to work out who they thought the werewolf was before the truth was revealed.

Nancy tumbled unhappily back to reality as the taxi approached St Benedict's College. Gothic turrets stood impassive against the bleak night sky. Not a soul to be found at the porter's lodge. Not a soul inside college at all, it seemed. St Benedict's had never felt more unwelcoming or more sinister. The indifferent moon bathed the fine brick elevations in an unhappy light and the stone eagles atop the north range seemed to signal down to her: 'Don't come in, unless you want to die.'

St Benedict's firs rocked like agitated lunatics beside the college lawn. The air was unpleasant, filled with the smell of decomposition, rot. Nancy opened the door to her room. Leon shivered as he crossed the threshold as if someone had just walked over his grave, as the saying goes. Nancy fetched a large canvas bag and began searching through unreliable towers of books. She put *Beloved*, *It*, and *The Haunting of Hill House* into the bag. She stopped mid-search and looked up at Leon anxiously. 'I don't have *Frankenstein* or The *Hellbound Heart*. They were from the library.'

'It's OK, I have them in my room.' Leon said gently.

Nancy didn't answer. She only opened and closed her mouth soundlessly, nodding towards the lawn.

A legion of dark figures is swarming across the grass. Ravening hunger contorts their deathly-white faces. They move oddly across the grass like so many faulty puppets. The women expose themselves suggestively. The men fight, fall, get up again. Here, then, are the vampires from *I Am Legend*, conjured by Leshi, in foul, infected hordes. Limbs flailing, voices appalling, they hurl themselves at the college entrance, beat the doors with their fists, break open the barred way. The two students run like hell, blindly, up, up. They sprint to Leon's room on the top floor and behind them, a siren call of screams answers the song of their desperate flight. The legion are closing in. Leon is at his door, dropping the keys he yanks from his trouser pocket.

'Hurry! 'Nancy shouts. 'They'll tear us apart!'

The siren call rises up in a raw, full-throated chorus: *Surrender to us; feed us; become us.*

Leon's hand shakes as he struggles to get the key in the lock, struggles to turn it; the damned lock was always so stiff! In fetid splendour, the legion arrive like a man who had often been chained hand and foot, but tears the chains apart and breaks the irons on his feet; like a man who cries out and cuts himself with stones, and when asked his name, replies, 'My name is Legion for we are many.' The legion arrive, corrupt and stinking, as Nancy and Leon slip through the door and slam it fast behind them.

The door resists the Sirens' deceit-filled song. *Surrender to us; feed us; become us.* The door dances on its hinges but holds for the moment.

Then the high screech of wood splintering.

Screws fly free from their hinges (sharp as darts). Jericho begins to fall.

Leon finds his desk in the dark, grabs his copies of *Frankenstein* and *The Hellbound Heart*. Nancy is at the window. Below, the gravel path is empty. The door cracks ajar; cadaverous fingers insinuate themselves between door and frame. Leon thrusts open the window. It is a long way down to the ground, a long way to fall. They will have to jump five, perhaps six, feet to the fire escape. The door screams open and the room is breached. In their wild hunger, the vampires fight, fall and trample one another. The confusion allows Nancy and Leon a few desperate seconds, perhaps all it takes to save a life.

'Go, now!' Leon says. 'I'm right behind you!'

Nancy hesitates briefly, then jumps for all she's worth. Her foot clips the handrail of the fire escape and she lands hard but safe on the iron platform. She shakes her head to clear it. Leon means to jump next but the vampires are already too many and it is already too late. He throws his books to Nancy; *Frankenstein* and *The Hellbound Heart* tumble through the air as if in slow-motion. He wonders if this is what dying is: the slow reduction of everything to an eternal stasis. Slow, slow, slower, slower, stopped. Cold arms enfold Leon in a blood-loving embrace. Nails rake at his flesh in search of the red wonder that pulls through his veins just under the surface. Everything burns. Everything reddens as the life of Leon Wilson runs out through tears in his skin. His death-scream is intolerable, all the world's error, misery and horror in a final exhalation. Nancy races to the bottom of the fire escape, 'don't trip, don't trip', taking the steps two at a time, 'don't trip, don't trip'. The final ladder is rusted tight and won't extend. She kicks it. She kicks it again. 'Come on!' The whole fire escape trembles under the weight of the legion behind her. *Surrender to us; feed us; become us.* 'Come on!' The ladder shrieks rustily and drops to the ground and she scrambles down it, hands shaking so violently, she falls. She picks up Leon's books and throws them into her bag; runs. The legion are streaming down the fire escape. *Surrender to us; feed us; become us.* Lightheaded with fear, she runs out through the college gates and onto the road. The legion swarm across the lawn. The taxi is waiting still.

Thank God! She throws herself onto the back seat.

'We need to go, now!' she says.

'All right, hold your horses.' The taxi driver is only half-listening; the radio is playing *Werewolves of London*. 'No need to panic,' he says, 'I didn't leave the meter running.'

'Please, we need to go. Look!' She turns to the rear window but the legion are gone. The taxi driver looks back at her, nonplussed.

'All right, Miss,' he says evenly, 'Pendleton Manor is it? What about the young man?'

'He's not coming,' Nancy says simply.

chapter twelve

"Again, she tried to take a breath, but it was as if her body had died, and she was staring out of it, unable now to breathe or blink or swallow."
THE HELLBOUND HEART | CLIVE BARKER

*Now, the inside could only be described
as wretched, raped, stripped bare.*

i

Like a church on a cliff top or a lighthouse on its rock, Pendleton Manor stood solidly against the sky. Completed by Lord Edward Pendleton in early autumn 1929 (just a few short weeks before the Wall Street Crash), the manor was intended as a symbol of the family's status and prosperity.

The Great Depression put paid to that, slowly and inexorably bankrupting the Pendletons. The grand exterior remained but the inside faded through neglect, and its treasures were sold to stave off ruin, if only temporarily.

Now there were no priceless Constables or

Waterhouses; no family portraits lining the grand staircase; no finely woven Persian carpets before monumental ornate fireplaces. Everything was sacrificed in service to the family's mounting debts. Now, the inside could only be described as wretched, raped, stripped bare.

Pendleton's wife died of tuberculosis. His twin sons, Alfred and William, were killed at the Battle of Normandy. Edward Pendleton became a misanthropic recluse and a dedicated inebriate. He died in the 1970s of alcoholism and left no survivor to inherit the estate. The manor fell into ruin, eaten away by weather, by ivy and ground elder, by rats and birds that became the new lords of the manor.

The house had seen every kind of depravity. Edward raped a scullery maid repeatedly in the weeks after his wife's death. Alfred and William bullied and viciously assaulted a gentle stable boy with a girlish manner. Collusion and deception covered up the truth about the boy's death. 'Eric Godley's skull was fractured fatally when he was kicked in the head by a horse,' read the coroner's report. (In truth, the fatal blow was struck by sixteen-year-old Alfred Pendleton with a hammer. But the Pendleton name had to be protected.)

Humanity as an experiment had failed at Pendleton Manor.

Not an ounce of warm blood ran through the veins of the Pendleton men. Between the shroud of skin and the hard Pendleton bones, no soul existed. Hence there was no warmth, no soul in Pendleton Manor itself. Nothing comes from nothing. Blood was spilled, vengeance planned, lies told, rape and murder perpetrated in this cruel and cunning house.

Humanity, as an experiment, has failed.

Can a house live? Can it gather evil to it? Can a house harbour resentment, develop a taste for the coldblooded cruelty that once drove its masters? Empty and alone, Pendleton Manor hungered for blood, corruption, revenge.

There will be black fire and red water and the earth turning and screaming...

The demon Leshi had found its way in, crawling through cracks, dry and crumbling, between bricks leaking dust into the wind. It had communed with the house, sympathised with it, promised it every possible contemptible act. Together – edifice and artifice – they would feast on the terror of anyone who set foot over the rotten threshold.

The demon harvested brutal feeling from the worst houses of all: the Marsten House (huge and rambling and like a ruined king); number 55 Lodovico Street (the blood-spangled floor); Seymour Hall (its chimney stacks dark silhouettes against the clear sky) and Hill House, of course, (whatever walked there, walked alone). The daily life of families and children, of cities and nations – all the touching, loving, interconnected fragmentedness of living – were to be destroyed in one night of disaster. Pendleton and Leshi – edifice and artifice – watched and waited.

ii

Obscured by an overgrown hedge of blackthorn run wild, the house was largely hidden from the road. Judy and Freya pulled wide the rusted iron gates, and drove into the grounds. The first thing Judy saw was a lone oak, gnarled and ancient, its thick branches spread out in a parody of welcome. Then she noticed the oddly disconcerting relationship between the house and the driveway. It was as if Pendleton were skulking in its own grounds, hidden from view like the proverbial spider waiting for a fly. The windows of the house were tall and beautiful but irretrievably damaged. Some of the panes were cracked, the frames rotten. Some were barricaded with steel sheets, garlanded with ugly graffiti. The untended flower beds were an opera of extremes – flowers and shrubs either wildly overgrown or the earth bare as desert through lack of water and care. Freya pulled up to the dilapidated portico and let the engine die. Judy anticipated something dark and stifling behind the great oak doors, something like gas in the atmosphere, the undetectable cause of their asphyxiation as soon as they stepped inside.

'Freya, look!' Judy pointed straight ahead. A red balloon drifted towards the car, tapped against the bonnet and sailed away up into the night sky, up, up, up to the edge of darkness itself.

'Come on,' Freya said, 'let's get this over with.' She left the keys swinging in the ignition and Judy pocketed them, picking up the strange little puzzle of Lemarchand's box. Together they carried the puzzle box, books, torches, and a petrol can to the house.

More headlights struck the gates, moving steadily towards the house, bathing the stonework in blank white light. The taxi's engine chunnered and shivered as Nancy got out and paid the driver. Judy found the rattly taxi strangely comforting, something normal to hold onto in the unfolding strangeness all around them.

The taxi moved off again; the driver glanced back

bemusedly at the three women standing in front of the dilapidated house. The cabbie drove out through the gates back into the outside world: a world of strolling by the Cam, grocery shopping at the market, curling up by the fireside with a good book.

'Where's Leon?' Freya asked.

'He's dead,' Nancy said flatly. 'Vampires. Hordes of them.'

'*I Am Legend*,' Freya murmured in acknowledgement.

iii

Next in our wicked little tale, a mist forms rapidly around the house like a shroud, cutting the women off from the outside world. Judy hears something in the middle distance, belligerent hollering or a perverse comedy act (she cannot tell which) advancing towards them and suddenly the legion are here, marching raggedly in the direction of the house.

'Do vampires look like that?' Judy says, pointing at the unholy mob.

'Get inside!' Freya yells.

The great oak doors are stiff to open but not locked; heavy to move, but not impossible. Freya, Judy and Nancy squeeze through the narrowest of gaps and heave the doors closed again behind them. They slide the heavy wooden bolt into position and the entrance is categorically locked and barred. The legion pound at the doors to be let in, crying out impotently that the three women should feed them, become them.

Then just as suddenly, there is silence.

The house sighs around them, a living, black-hearted

thing. Freya's torch finds broken and upended flagstones; worm-eaten panelling; a teetering Venus de Milo. Judy and Nancy follow behind and the friends penetrate the manor's innards. Massive double doors reveal the dining room: ornate chairs with broken backs and faded seats, some upturned; a silver candelabra strung with cobwebs atop a long, dust-furred mahogany table. Freya places the books carefully in a circle on the table; Judy sees them all together for the first time: stories of killer clowns, plague-ridden rats, lascivious werewolves, murdered children who come back from the dead. She feels a sharp stab of guilt; she has read these books; she is culpable because she could not resist horror's morbid little itch; she had come to desire the insufferable horror, the Hitchcockian moment, the wild and barely tolerable frisson of fear. All of them had fed their fear to this cunning, hungry thing. It had feasted vicariously on pages smeared with blood and terror; a king's banquet of depravity and death.

Everyone's entitled to at least one good scare; the masked man at the window; the creature in the woods; the bump in the attic but Judy was afraid of the extent of human feeling, of what other horrors lay hidden in the depths of the human heart. She followed Freya's instructions mechanically, soaking the perimeter of the room with petrol, extending the line of fuel all the way out into the corridor. Freya charged the candelabra with tall candles retrieved from the bottom of her bag and lit them ceremoniously. Once the candelabra was ablaze, she placed Lemarchand's box in the centre of the circle of books. She held out her hands to Judy and Nancy. Instinctively, each took the hand she was offered.

For I am the Lord your God who takes hold of your right

hand and says to you, Do not fear; I will help you.

'What next?' Judy whispered .

'I'm going to summon Leshi,' Freya said, 'then we light the petrol and run.'

'Are you sure this is going to work?' asked Nancy.

'No, I'm not,' Freya said, giving both their hands a reassuring squeeze.

'Leshi, I summon you,' Freya began. 'Reveal yourself to me, not as a wolf, nor as a raven, nor as a towering tree, but as I command.' Freya is ancient witch-goddess again. The green man is in the woods. Blue stones fly from Wales to Salisbury plain. Base metals turn into gold. Her voice quavers a little because of her hammering heart. Something whispers slyly in the room, lifting dust from the floor. Ash falls in the fireplace like rustling leaves in an unholy tomb.

'I summon you, Leshi.'

An animal stench fills the room.

'Reveal yourself to me, not as a wolf.'

In the distance, a bell begins to toll.

'Not as a raven, nor as a towering tree, but as I command!'

Here it comes, you bastard, here it is, leech. Here it is for you.

Freya turns, squeezing Judy's hand so tightly, Judy struggles to stop herself from crying out. Judy and Nancy follow Freya's gaze to Lemarchand's box, rising into the air, segments of the puzzle sliding open to reveal its cyphered interior.

Abruptly it falls.

The bell stops tolling.

In the snow-drift quiet, a far more terrible sound: something dragging itself along the corridor.

'Cenobites?' Nancy says.

A shadow falls across the open doorway, the shadow of those who mourn, the shadow of those without hope, the shadow of those without a friend in the world. Freya, Nancy and Judy understand this all too well because the shadow belongs to a woman known to them all.

They have studied her mind, and her madness. She has been there since the beginning, since Judy Miller first walked into Persephone's and this fills all three women with unspeakable dread. Now, almost inevitably, everything has come full circle. It is Leshi's little jest; a humorous sleight-of-hand; one final, killing joke.

She is in her early thirties, or maybe, as it says, no more no less than thirty-two; she is fanciful and isolated; awkward in the world, unsure of who she is. She has been waiting for just this moment. She is perfect in her desperation, she is perfectly lonely, she is perfect in her need for love – but love from whom? – from her beloved Theodora, of course.

She looks at all three, but there is only one she really sees: Judy Miller, the ingenue in a world of horror. She draws her own name from Judy's lips.

'Eleanor,' Judy whispers.

'Theodora, is it really you?' the shadow-woman Eleanor says, so very sweetly, in return.

Whatever walked there, walked alone.

The nightmare in the room is Eleanor Vance, hero (anti-hero?) of *The Haunting of Hill House* by Shirley Jackson. For her whole life, ever since first memory, Eleanor had been waiting for something like Hill House.

So now we have the final act; inspired by a book that Judy Miller picked up one autumn afternoon and read by her cosy fireside at 94 Eden Street, Cambridge CB1; a place she may never see again.

It is the book she was clutching when she first took her place at the Shirley Jackson Club.

The book was in her hand the day she sat opposite Preet, first heard about 'the boys': Leon and Tom. All three of those young lives lost among the bloodied pages of Daphne du Maurier, Stephen King, Richard Matheson, Mary Shelley, Angela Carter and, of course, dear horror lover, the ineluctable Shirley Jackson.

Nancy lets go of Freya's hand, no Cenobites have come to tear her soul apart. This is how it could all end, or Nancy Yamada may just be the person to end it.

Black anger like she's never felt before darkens her vision: she must have vengeance for the death of her friends. She swings the burning candelabra as hard as she can at Eleanor Vance but Eleanor merely flinches. No more, no less than that.

Eleanor retaliates, striking Nancy hard on the side of the head, hurling her against the wall with such unnatural force that Nancy is knocked unconscious and slumps to the floor. A fallen candle rolls across the petrol-sodden floor and how rapidly the flames leap and lick and run from one end of the room to the other. Everything is dancing yellows and blues, twisting, turning and turning again. Freya tries to help Nancy up. Eleanor seizes her by the throat so that she hangs in the air, thrashing and gasping. Judy tries to intervene but Eleanor jettisons her across the room with a dismissive toss of the arm. The car keys jangle onto the floor. Judy looks up to see Freya's face blanch, close to the edge, almost passing out, surrendering.

'Eleanor!' Judy shouts, trying frantically to remember

the details of *Hill House*, the story of Eleanor and Theodora. 'Nell,' Judy says, 'my poor little Nell. Come with me, Nell. We'll go away together. That's what you want, isn't it?'

Eleanor's brow wrinkles as if she is trying to remember something. She lets Freya fall to the ground with the sound of bone knocking on wood. Smoke is filling the room now as the fire feasts on a banquet of oxygen.

'Judy, don't!' Freya hisses. 'You know how this ends.'

'It's the only way,' Judy says softly. 'I am really doing this.'

Now she has become the pages of the book, the ink, the paper, the word made flesh. 'Come with me, Nell,' Judy says, picking up the car keys. 'We can go now. You've only got one suitcase.'

'I don't want to go away from here,' Eleanor says.

'But you can't stay,' Judy says, 'not without me, Nell.' Eleanor Vance flushes darkly and Judy runs like the Devil. She runs out into the corridor, clambers out of a shattered window, cutting her hands on broken glass, runs and runs until she reaches the little Beetle, not daring to look back. She puts the key into the ignition, terrified of the demon wearing the face of Eleanor Vance. The engine roars into life.

One last shout for good versus evil.

'I was happy,' she thinks as the blood roars in her ears. 'I have been happy.'

Now a heavy thump on the roof of the car; the demon scratches at the roof as Judy pulls away.

I am really doing it.

'I will not go away from here!' Eleanor cries. 'I will not go!'

'Yes you will!' Judy retorts. 'You must!'

'You can't get rid of me,' Eleanor-Leshi-Eleanor laughs. 'You brought me here.'

'And now I say you have to go!'

Judy puts her foot down and the wheels spin hard. The windscreen shatters like so many stars. Leshi-Eleanor grabs wildly at Judy. The car swerves like a Keystone Cops comedy – except it is unfunny – and Judy is searching for the giant oak.

Where is that damned tree?

I am doing this all by myself.

'Get out! Get out now!' The voice is Sebastian's. 'This is all my fault. I have to be the one to make it right.'

In case you were wondering, the narrative-gods (aka *William* Jackson) have hidden Sebastian on the VW's back seat (like a good B-movie villain) until his moment for heroics arrives.

It has arrived.

Sebastian reaches for the door handle, musters all his strength and shoves Judy from the speeding car, sends her away from certain death back into life.

The world is spinning and Judy is tumbling in the rough, damp grass. A sharp crack, followed by molten pain, tells her she has fractured her wrist. But she is alive. She turns her head weakly to see the VW Beetle careen into the great oak tree. The cracking thunder of bent and broken metal. The explosion is bright. The flames shoot high into the blackest of skies.

iv

Sebastian Sizemore, successful author of mass market, pulp horror paperbacks is dead. Something deep in Judy's soul tells her that Leshi is gone too. The night will give way to a new, more hopeful dawn. The universe will say 'thank you' to the old oak for its service and for its patience in the long wait before it was able to fulfil its destiny.

But the real miracle of this night has not yet taken place. Here it is in the shape of a young man approaching Judy.

Leon!

His face is beaten and scratched. His left eye is swollen and purplish. He's limping a little. He helps Judy up and she winces, 'My wrist,' she says hoarsely, 'it's almost certainly broken.'

'You'll live,' he says.

'I thought you were dead.'

'The legion wanted the books, not me.'

Orange flames add a premature sunrise to the night sky. Smoke rises from the sorry hulk of Pendleton Manor behind Nancy and Freya as they make their way slowly to the others. Freya sighs at the burning remains of her little Beetle. 'Oh dear!'

'Sebastian was in the car,' Judy says. 'He saved me.'

'He righted his wrongs,' Freya says quietly, 'as far as he was able.' She touches Judy's cheek with the tenderness of a careworn but committed lover. 'We need to get that wrist looked at.'

'Is it over now?' Judy asks her. 'Is Leshi gone for good?'

'Yes,' Freya says. 'I believe it is.'

V

Behind them the flames leap higher, eating Pendleton Manor alive. And the city of Cambridge, if it cared to look in that direction, would witness, but not mourn, the manor's showy demise. By morning, Pendleton, once pernicious and vengeful, will be a smoking husk.

When the ash settles and the blackness of the night comes again, something will stir there, oh-so-faintly. Silence will draw its veil over ruined brick and stone. Something will look out at the world from where doors and windows once stood. And that something has all the words and images of *Frankenstein, The Bloody Chamber, The Hellbound Heart* and, of course, *The Haunting of Hill House,* to keep it company on its lonely vigil.

For whatever darkness walked inside there, walks there still. And whatever walks there, walks alone.

epilogue

"We are on a tiny island in a raging sea; we are a point of safety in a world of ruin."
THE SUNDIAL | SHIRLEY JACKSON

The Gods were giving the city of Cambridge a show:
a fanfare for the future on a lazy summer afternoon.

Fiery ginger, the fleeting tartness of cranberry, the tang of orange on the tongue – Cambridge Tiffin was a dense and luxurious vice – and a Bridges café favourite. Outside Apollo was dancing in a cerulean sky, sending down his blessings into every corner of the city. Life is good again, thought Judy as she popped the last remaining chunk of tiffin into her mouth.

'This is far better than the manuscript I read,' Freya said, tapping the proof copy of Sebastian Sizemore's latest, and last, novel, *The Devil's Siren*. Alicia Brightwell, heroine of *The Devil's Maidens* and *The Devil's Mistress*, returns as a nightclub singer on the verge of a promising pop career – except a band of Satanists are eager to wed her, in blood sacrifice, with their lord and master. The cover showed a young woman with abundant tresses of blonde hair, singing suggestively into a microphone as a group of hooded figures watched from the shadows. *Lurid* was the word. Beneath the title, the legend, 'The final thrilling novel from England's grand master of horror,' was emblazoned in scarlet. 'I read it in one sitting. Absolutely unputdownable.'

Judy dabbed her lips with her napkin. 'How come it's so different from the original version?' she asked.

'Maybe the great Shirley Jackson worked on it in secret, put her inimitable stamp on it.'

Judy raised an eyebrow. 'I hope this means dear old Sebastian will be back on the bestseller lists with a posthumous hit.'

'Very probably.' Freya tossed the book onto the table. 'You should have a read of it.'

'I think I'll give horror a rest for a while.' Judy chuckled, massaging her wrist.

'Is it still giving you trouble?' Freya asked.

'Now and again,' Judy said. 'Have you heard from Leon or Nancy?'

'They're thinking of getting a flat-share together in the autumn but right now they're swatting up like crazy for their exams.' Freya paused. 'They've said 'yes' to starting the Shirley Jackson Club up again, maybe in October. Fancy coming along?'

'I think I've had enough scares to last a lifetime.'

Freya reached across the table and placed a warm hand over Judy's. 'Leshi is definitely gone.' Judy looked away as if searching for something.

And there, standing in the blazing sunshine by the iron gates of St John's College, was a clown. His face was painted stark white. There were funny tufts of red hair on either side of his bald head. A big clown-smile was painted over his mouth. He was holding an array of brightly-coloured balloons.

'Look!' Judy said. Children were running towards the clown, encircling him. He knelt down and began to divide the balloons amongst small, eager hands.

'No need to worry,' Freya laughed. 'Just a man in a clown suit entertaining the tourists. Probably promoting a local event.' But Judy wasn't really listening; her eyes were fixed on a solitary red balloon, floating down the street. It glided along in an oddly intentional way, as if searching for something, or someone. It moved across the window of the café, tapping against the surface of the glass, then it flew away on the warm breeze. Judy looked at Freya uncertainly. 'It's nothing, honestly,' Freya said. 'Just one that got away from our friend in the clown suit.' She drained her coffee and pushed back her chair decisively. 'Come on, let's go for a stroll on Jesus Green.'

Journeys end in lovers meeting.

Freya took Judy's hand and they walked along Portugal Place, past the Parish Church of St Clement, founded over a thousand years earlier, dedicated to St Clement, patron saint of mariners. The present church was fashioned out of rubble in the middle of the 13th Century, a silent witness to the Black Death, the English Civil War, the Industrial Revolution, two world wars, free love and flower power. Each came and went, leaving their marks on the city; some visible, some invisible, all indelible.

Freya and Judy made their way onto Park Parade. A large crowd had gathered on the grass of Jesus Green. People were looking upwards, some holding small children who pointed wide-eyed at the sky.

Hundreds and hundreds of red balloons were lifting gracefully into the sky, rising above the treetops, drifting high over the city's houses in the Kite, Petersfield and New Town, drifting over Jesus College, St John's, Trinity, and the rest; out beyond The Backs to Fen Coe and Grantchester Meadows. For a second, Freya caught sight of a stout, middle-aged woman with cat-eye glasses and hair tied neatly back. The woman stared at them directly for an instant then melted into the crowd. The people were turning now to look behind them and Judy and Freya did the same: in the distance more balloons were drifting skywards, high above the Fitzwilliam and the Botanical Gardens. In their thousands now, the red balloons dotted the blue of the sky, brilliant vermillion on a pointillist's canvas. The gods were giving the city of Cambridge a show; a fanfare for the future on a lazy summer afternoon; a line emphatically drawn under a tumultuous past. Freya slung her arm around Judy and they both began to laugh.

Trip no further, pretty sweeting, journeys end in lovers meeting.

Fin

Coming 2026

Satan's Blood

The sequel to *Satan's Lamp*

William Jackson

2027

The Shirley Jackson Club

will return in

The Medusa File

William Jackson

Cambridge Queer Press

❧

Image credits:

Cover: Lisa from Pexels
https://www.pexels.com/photo/10034029

Page 18: Ricky Esquivel
https://www.pexels.com/photo/1907784

Page 38: Magda Ehlers
https://www.pexels.com/photo/2573440

Page 54: Cottonbro Studio
https://www.pexels.com/photo/4874507

Page 72: Lisa from Pexels
https://www.pexels.com/photo/13920270

Page 90: Pixabay
https://www.pexels.com/photo/33083

Page 110: Giovanni
https://www.pexels.com/photo/21953337

Page 128: KoolShooters
https://www.pexels.com/photo/6494658

Page 148: Cottonbro Studio
https://www.pexels.com/photo/5427546

Page 164: Alena Darmel
https://www.pexels.com/photo/6940241

Page 184: Darya Chervatyuk
https://www.pexels.com/photo/2554743

Page 202: Cottonbro Studio
https://www.pexels.com/photo/5435560

Page 216: Ekaterina Astakhova
https://www.pexels.com/photo/4138721

Page 232: Jakub Pabis
https://www.pexels.com/photo/10519596